Like
Porno for
Psychos

Wrath James White

deadite press

DEADITE PRESS
205 NE BRYANT
PORTLAND, OR 97211
www.DEADITEPRESS.com

AN ERASERHEAD PRESS COMPANY
www.ERASERHEADPRESS.com

ISBN: 1-936383-84-5

All stories copyright © 2011 Wrath James White

Cover art copyright © 2011 Suzzan Blac
www.SUZZANB.com

All rights reserved. No part of this book may be reproduced or transmitted in any form or by any means, electronic or mechanical, including photocopying, recording, or by any information storage and retrieval system, without the written consent of the publisher, except where permitted by law.

Printed in the USA.

To Mom

DEADITE PRESS BOOKS BY WRATH JAMES WHITE
The Book of a Thousand Sins
Population Zero
His Pain

CONTENTS

SEX AND SLAUGHTER

How can you say I do not love you
merely because I am destructive
in the expression of my love?

I love you
as only the starving wolf
can love the wounded deer
with an obsessive adoration
like physical hunger.

It is to adore them forever
uninterrupted
that I would pinch off your eyelids
to never be denied the spectacle
of your wondrous eyes.

It is to never see your lovely smile
deceased from your face
that I would pull up the corners
of your full red lips
and pin them to your cheeks.

It is so your voluptuous breasts

would never succumb to age or gravity
that I would bind them in piano wire
and anchor them to your throat.

And so you would never forget
the sensation of my mouth
wet hot against the joining of your thighs
and I
never to forget the taste
that I would cannibalize your sex
savage your labia and clitoris
with my teeth
chew up into your ovaries.

And how could mere malice
or cowardly misogyny
explain such an act?
Only love can rationalize this madness
this passion
which even now brings the taste of your sex
melting on my tongue like a sweet confection
to my tastebuds
and tears of the most profound joy
to my adoring eyes.

LIKE PEYOTE
FOR PIMPS

Cocoa's face was covered in livid purple bruises. Her front teeth had been completely shattered and her nose was smeared across her face as if she'd gone twelve rounds with a heavyweight. Her neck bore the marks of ligature strangulation. The finger saw the perpetrator used to murder her was still embedded in her esophagus. A hideous gaping wound yawned open beneath her chin like a blood-soaked second smile. The serrated wire had cut straight through to her vertebrae, nearly decapitating her. Coagulated blood formed a tremendous pool all around her. Her tank top and miniskirt had been pulled up and her bra and panties were missing. One of her breasts looked like it had been chewed up. If G hadn't paid for it himself, he'd never have been able to tell that her clothes were once white. G turned his head as shivers began to raise goosebumps all over his skin. That's all he could stand to look at. The rest of the damage was just too horrible. He shoved the picture across the table, back toward the detective.

"This is the second ho you've lost this week, Tyson. Is this how you protect your girls?"

"Pimpin' ain't easy," hissed the leather-clad, platinum and diamond bejeweled pimp in a voice that was low and raspy from too much alcohol and weed. It was one of those universally excepted truisms of the game, so self-evident as to hardly merit repeating. Tyson Price (better known as G-Town Slim) first heard the age-old axiom from the lips of his father. He would mutter it everyday in an exhausted sigh as he collapsed onto the lambskin leather couch and rolled himself a joint after kicking G's mother out of the house to work the Boulevard for tricks. When G's mother was murdered by a trick who gave her AIDS back in '83, he remembers hearing his dad mutter those same words over her grave before sliding into the back of his block-long Lincoln Town Car with his new ho and disappearing from G's life forever. G was only eight years old then. Almost two decades later, he was a mirror image of his dad.

G-town Slim wore a full-length leather coat, a silk Armani shirt, and tight Hugo Boss jeans with a pair of snakeskin boots. His neck, ears, and wrist were iced with a sparkling platinum necklace hung with a six-inch crucifix, 2 Karat diamond earrings, and a diamond encrusted platinum Rolex from Jacob the jeweler. He made this detective's monthly salary in one night on the streets. Still, he wished he could have traded places with him at that moment.

The cop shoved the photo back at him, grabbing him by his soft brown dreadlocks and forcing his head down onto the table, rubbing his face into the photo, forcing him to look closer at the ruin done to Cocoa's privates. Her vagina had been completely eaten away. Her murderer chewed away all her labia and clitoris leaving one ragged hole. He had completely cannibalized her sex. G-town threw up all over the desk.

Pimpin' ain't easy. Some days however, were worse than others.

The detectives let Tyson go. Apparently regurgitation wasn't the common response of sex murderers when confronted with evidence of their crimes. Selena, one of

G's main money-makers, picked him up at the station in his money green Mercedes E-class. She immediately began chattering on about a new ultra slim smart-phone she wanted that did everything but suck dick and give handjobs. When her incessant squawking grew too much for him to tolerate, he quieted her with a slap. The silence immediately rushed in and began to work his nerves even worse than Selena's high-pitched whine. There were too many questions coiled like serpents within the quiet, waiting to strike and constrict. He could feel his lungs slowly crushing beneath their weight.

He turned on the radio and blasted a frenetic hip-hop tune with indecipherable lyrics spit out like machine gun fire in an exaggerated southern drawl. It didn't help. He could still see Cocoa's battered and vandalized corpse in his mind, competing with the memory of her head banging against the roof of the Mercedes as he'd given her a little something to remember him by last night before putting her out on the stroll. He wasn't concerned about his semen showing up inside her during the autopsy. He always used a condom. Besides, he never denied that she was his ho. It would be no surprise that he would have fucked her, but fucking a girl was a far cry from doing to her what he had seen in those pictures.

G-town felt himself slipping into a depression as he recalled the image of his beautiful Cocoa, with her platinum blonde hair and smooth milk chocolate skin, ripped open and looted of her most valuable parts. Her lovely breasts with the big perky nipples like Hershey Kisses were still fresh in his mind, how they'd tasted the night before and how they'd appeared in that photo with one of the nipples bitten off. He reached under the seat and grabbed the bottle of French La Bleue, an imported French Absinthe, that he'd acquired a habit for at the last Player's Ball in New Orleans. Almost choking, he took a long swig from the bottle and grimaced as the fiery green liquid burned its way down his throat. Then he lit up his "special" joint, a marijuana cigarette mixed with opium leaves. The same pimp who turned him onto La Bleue had turned him out on opium and weed. It was a high that made you never want to land.

It was at the fifteenth annual Player's Ball in New Orleans. An old pimp who called himself Hundred Dollar Bill and still maintained a stable of nearly thirty women introduced the exotic inhalant to him as they watched the whores compete in a striptease to see who was the best "Bottom Bitch" in the West. While naked prostitutes undulated on the floor and dry humped each other, Hundred Dollar Bill pulled out a fat sack of weed and another of dried opium leaves and began mixing the two together on a CD cover of James Brown's greatest hits. He cut open a White Owl cigar with a switchblade, dumped the tobacco out into an ashtray, then rolled the opium and marijuana up in the cigar paper while extolling the virtues of the pungent cigar to G-Town.

"Forget all that cocaine and heroine and ecstasy and junk. That stuff don't do nothing but make you stupid. I mean, that's all cool to impress the ladies, but this here is the bomb. This is the real pimp shit. Brother, this will put the ice in your game. How do you think I'm able to hold down a stable when I'm damned near sixty years old? Because I'm a visionary. It was my idea to start sellin' pussy over the internet. This here is where I get my visions. The Native Americans have peyote, Timothy Leary introduced acid to the white boys, to the pimp, the spirits of our ancestors speak to us through the chronic. Now lace it with a little of this opium and the effects are ten-fold. Man, a couple hits of this and you can see eternity and it is sweet, my brother. It is so sweet." He took a long draw on the over-stuffed joint and passed it to G-town.

"Like peyote for pimps, huh?" G asked, as he turned it

over in his hands.

"Something like that, yeah. It helps a brotha see the truth beneath reality. See, cause that's where a pimp lives— beneath reality, in its disease infected bowels. This here helps you negotiate through the sewers."

With only a modest stable of six girls, G-town deferred to the wisdom of his more successful elder and began indulging regularly of the hallucinogenic weed. He was hooked after the first night spent watching the room spin and whores twist and contort like images in a funhouse mirror. They wound up spending the night together. Retiring to a four-star hotel suite with the best hoes from their collective stables. For a man in his late fifties, the old pimp fucked like a teenager. He of course attributed his stamina to the weed. He said it made every experience more intense. Tonight however, all it seemed to do was make the horrible images of Cocoa's savaged corpse more vivid, adding details to it that he hadn't been aware of before. Like the way her eyes were half-lidded and a sly smile seemed to stretch across her bruised and battered face as if she'd just had a really good orgasm or smoked some bomb-ass weed herself.

G pulled the Mercedes to a halt at the corner of Broad Street and Spruce where his other two whores were busy getting money. He gave Selena two tabs of xstasy and a long hit off his joint before kicking her out onto the sidewalk. They always felt special when he let them hit from his joint. He told each of his ladies that it was a privilege only granted to them and that he would kick the shit out of them if they told and made the other girls jealous. They knew he was full of shit, but they liked the way the weed made them feel when combined with the Xstasy. It almost made them *want* to fuck the sweaty, overweight, undesirables that lined up to punch their pathetic erections into the girl's distended orifices each night.

"Now go get my money, bitch," G cooed affectionately,

planting a long slow kiss on Selena's lips and trying not to think of how many cocks she'd sucked with that mouth. Most women would do just about anything with their mouths that a trick paid them to do except kiss them. That was just too intimate. That was the one thing they reserved for their man and any pimp who refused to kiss his whores, no matter how many buckets of cum she'd sucked down that night, would soon find himself whoreless. It was one of the prices a playa had to pay to be part of the game.

He tasted the minty flavor of mouthwash and was grateful that she'd remembered. All of his whores carried mouthwash and douche in their bags. The type of tricks who paid two hundred dollars an hour didn't want to smell a woman's profession on her breath or when she spread her legs.

"You sure you don't want me to take care of you first, Daddy? You look like you could use some of this good Puerto Rican pussy right now."

"All I want from you, bitch is two thousand dollars before sunrise. You hear me?"

"Yes, Daddy."

G-town swallowed a capsule of X and watched Selena's tight voluptuous ass bounce off down the street, enveloped in black leather. He felt his dick stiffen in his pants as he remembered how well she could work that miraculous calypigian.

Maybe I could have used some of that fine Spanish pussy after all. He thought. Maybe busting a nut in her perfect ass would have cleared the cobwebs from his head and put some sunshine back into his thoughts. It was too late now. He would look weak to the other girls and they'd get jealous if he pulled her in off the boulevard for a quick fuck. He'd have to wait until the end of the night when she was done getting his paper.

G sat there on the corner for nearly an hour, watching

Selena and his two other hoes Yolanda and Tina turn tricks like they were born to the task. They always worked harder when they knew he was watching. He knew that if he wasn't there they'd probably be slipping into the alley to smoke weed and snort coke or they'd spend an extra twenty minutes with some trick, telling him their fucking life story instead of giving him the pussy, getting his money, and getting the fuck back out on the stroll.

He nearly finished an entire bottle of La Bleue as he watched his girls prey on the male sexual appetite to his economic advantage. It was a good night. The tricks were biting and G could almost see the dollars stacking up. Still, he was short two hoes now, and that meant less money no matter how you sliced it.

As if it wasn't hard enough for an honest pimp to earn a living, now he had this mess to deal with, some lunatic murdering his product. Fate wasn't content to make his life miserable by having the cops bust his hoes just for standing on the corner too long or shaking them down for free pussy. It wasn't bad enough that the other pimps were always trying to pull hoes from his stable. There were tricks raping, robbing and sometimes killing his moneymakers. Then there were the usual obstacles of hoes getting pregnant, drug addicted, falling in love with a trick or just getting so lazy he had to break his leg off in their ass on a regular basis just to keep his money from getting funny. And now there was something out there eating his bitches. This was the last thing that G-town needed.

The night before they'd found his bottom bitch and main money-maker, Desiree' "White Chocolate" Williams, with most of her female anatomy cannibalized and now Cocoa was gone too. G had tried to put a spin on it with his remaining girls to keep them from getting scared and running.

"Now, I know y'all miss Desiree'. I'm gonna miss that

bitch too. And not just for the four gees a night she was pullin' down. She was the first hoe I pulled in this town and she'll always have a special place in my heart. But she was too stuck on the cunnilingus. She probably tried to get some pimp to eat that sweet pussy of hers and he got mad and sicked a pit-bull on her ass or something. I done told ya'll to steer clear of those other pimps. They catch you even looking at them and they'll try to claim you. I know it's a hard lesson, but y'all got to learn that pussy-eatin' is for the tricks and the other hoes in the stable. Ain't no pimp gonna go for that shit. Not even with his bottom hoe. Y'all bitches don't know how well y'all got it with me. Man, there's some hardcore gorilla pimps out there that'll cut a bitch up just for talkin' some shit like that."

It was obvious the girls accepted his explanation reluctantly, skeptical of his reasoning. But G-town knew that by the time they were ready to hit the stroll again, they would have convinced themselves that he was right. It was the only way they'd be able to face the streets and they had no choice in that matter. It was either the streets or the back of G-town's hand. Of course, they didn't know about Cocoa yet. They would trip when they found out another one of G's girls had been eaten. And G-town knew something none of his girls knew yet, that Desiree' and Cocoa had not been the only girls attacked by that lunatic.

Cadillac Jim lost a girl just two nights ago. They found her with her breasts and snatch eaten away and her throat torn out. And Platinum K lost two of his hoes last weekend. They'd both been found with breasts, vagina, and buttocks completely consumed.

But G-town couldn't let any of that mess with his money. He had a 500 dollar a night cocaine habit and a taste for French La Bleue, fine clothes, expensive cars, and opium and marijuana that went into the tens of thousands. He couldn't allow some pussy-hungry, psycho werewolf trick to stop the flow of Benjamins.

G pulled another bottle of Absinthe from the glove compartment and began working on it. By the time the black van pulled up in front of Selena, G-town was somewhere over the rainbow.

He didn't know if it was the opium or the absinthe, but the man behind the wheel of the van had a face that seemed to morph in and out between a piranha and a gigantic vagina with teeth. He stared at the hideous thing as it beckoned to Selena and wondered why she would even consider getting into the car with a freak like that.

Can't she tell that pussy-face is the killer? The one who's been eating whores out fuckin' literally? That ho has no sense at all.

G rolled down the window and shouted for her, but it was too late. She disappeared into the van and it sped off down the street. G-town started up the Mercedes and followed them. He couldn't afford to lose another moneymaker.

The van drove down Spruce Street, across Broad Street, and then made a left onto 11th and another left onto Walnut. It drove a few more blocks before coming to rest in an alley beside an old recently renovated Colonial row-home. They got out and the man's face was that of a piranha again. Two other girls got out of the van with them. Apparently, one girl was not enough. The man had a big appetite. Still, Selena was the best looking of the bunch and the man seemed acutely aware of that fact.

His eyes were huge and seemed to be lasciviously devouring Selena's image. The rows of razor sharp teeth glistened and his gills undulated. Selena giggled and took his hand as he led her from the van into the alley and then from the alley into his house. G-town parked the E-class and followed behind. He still had the fat joint clutched between his teeth, smoking it like it was a cigarette.

There were no blinds on the tiny window in the kitchen door so he was able to watch everything they were doing from where he stood in the alley. The fish-headed trick wasn't wasting anytime. He sent the other two whores on into the living room and kept Selena behind. He immediately began ripping her clothing off in a haphazard fury, like a child unwrapping presents on Christmas day. When her naked flesh was finally revealed, the piranha's eyes glazed with a carnivorous lust. His serrated teeth glistened with some slimy goo that Selena still appeared oblivious to. She kissed him... right on those big fishy lips. G reminded himself to put his foot in her ass for that.

It finally occurred to G that perhaps the man's face was really not that of a huge piranha or a rapacious vagina. Selena was a nasty freak, but even she wouldn't kiss something that looked like that and no way Desiree' and Cocoa would have gotten into a van with a mutant land shark. Maybe it was the opium allowing him to see through to the man's soul. It was the only thing that made sense. Knowing the images he was seeing were not real did nothing to dispel them however. He watched in horror as the thing lowered its head between Selena's thighs and began to feed.

He was gentle at first; lapping at her clitoris with lavish attention. His eyes swam in his head as if he was in a delirious rapture. Selena's did too. He plunged a thick fat tongue that looked like some type of slimy pink sea slug up into her cunt and began fucking her with it, sliding it in and out and then flicking it across her swollen clitoris. Selena began to moan and scream as an orgasm built within her and then exploded, tossing her body into violent convulsions so furious it looked as if she would inadvertently snap her own neck or spinal cord. That's when the piranha's appetite got the better of him. G saw it coming a second before he sunk those hideous razor sharp teeth into Selena's sweet vagina and began ripping off her labia, devouring them like some romantic fool plucking rose pedals. *She loves me. She loves me not.* The trick's eyes shined with a hunger that defied reason as he consumed her salacious flower, burrowing between her thighs and chewing his way up inside her. Selena screamed and thrashed and beat at him, but he was too strong and she couldn't shake him free.

"Motherfucker!" G exclaimed, letting the joint slip from his lips onto the floor. He broke down the door and staggered into the room with his shiny black Glock .40 pointed at the piranha's head. Only now it looked like a pussy again and Selena looked like a blow up doll with exceptionally large vibrating orifices.

"Get your filthy hands off my ho!" G could barely hold the gun steady as the room began to swirl around him. He had to focus to keep the two in his sights. He had drunk way too much.

"Hello, son," the piranha spoke, grinning from ear to ear with his gore-streaked maw, bloody strips of Selena's vagina still drooling from between his fanged teeth.

"Back away from her!"

"Don't you know who I am son?"

"I don't know you, fool! A guy with a head that looks like a vagina with teeth? I don't know no muthafuckas as ugly as you!"

"That's the Absinthe talkin'. Look deeper. You know me, Tyson."

"How did you know my name?"

"Look deeper."

G stared at the man's hideous countenance as he continued to chew. The man's face lost its cohesion and began to run like melting lard. The piranha/pussy face fell away and the face beneath it swam into view. Now, G recognized him.

"Hundred Dollar Bill! You're that old pimp from New

Orleans, right? The one that hipped me to La Bleue?"

"Yeah son, but I'm more than that. Look deeper, Tyson."

G-town stared at the old wrinkled brown face, the bushy eyebrows and goatee that were now almost completely white, the shaved head. Then he stared into the man's cold black eyes. It was the eyes that gave him away. G remembered looking into those eyes while his own filled with tears, watching them stare down into his mother's grave without a hint of remorse. He remembers seeing those eyes look back at him as he stood beside his mother's tombstone watching his father drive away.

"Dad?"

The other whores came into the room now. They'd heard Selena's screaming stop and figured it was time for them to earn their paper. They took one look at Selena's ruined sex, the piranha's blood-soaked whiskers, and G-town's gun and began to scream. The piranha grabbed both of them by their throats, abruptly choking off their nerve-wracking shrieks, and turned back around to face G.

"But why? Why are you killing these girls? Why the fuck are you killing my bitches?"

"It's about the power of creation, son, the power of a god! They have it and we don't. What I'm doing here is taking communion, ingesting the very essence of creation. The pussy. The womb. The universe is in here, son. This ain't just pussy here, boy. It's heaven. It's the motherfuckin' house of God!"

"You are fucking crazy, old man!"

"And you are just not high enough yet. Smoke some more." He nodded toward the joint that sat on the kitchen counter already rolled and waiting and G walked over and picked it up.

"Smoke, son. You'll see. We'll take communion together, as father and son, the way God intended."

Tyson Price aka G-town Slim, lit up the fat cigar filled with opium and marijuana and put it between his lips, inhaling deeply. This joint was twice as strong as the ones he rolled and he was already so high that this last hit nearly knocked him unconscious. In fact, he wasn't sure if he was still conscious or not. He could feel the world reel and tilt like he was in a dream. Everything began to dissolve and fly asunder. The girls no longer looked like whores. They didn't even look human. They looked like eternity. They looked like all of nature compressed into two single forms and at their center swirled a maelstrom of energy, power, creation ... right between their legs. The nexus of all realities.

"Ah, you see it now." His father cooed seductively.

The two whores were scared to death and were still staring at the gun in G-town's hand. They relaxed visibly when he dropped the gun. Then they tensed again when they heard Selena moan. She was still alive and in pain. The old man released the two girls and snatched a roll of copper wire from the kitchen counter and wrapped it around Selena's throat. He began to strangle her as G stood watching in a narcotic stupor.

"Now, son! Before the light goes out!"

G looked down at the ragged hole his father had chewed in Selena's sex, in that good Puerto Rican pussy. He could see a glow there, like a sunrise, moonlight and stars. He felt a hunger surge within him. The hunger to become one with her, with everything. He knelt down and began to feed, first on her breasts and then on the remains of her sex. The two whores began screaming again. They ran back into the house. G rose from between Selena's thighs as her body began to convulse in spastic death throes that resembled orgasm.

"I can see it! I can see God!" G exclaimed as he rose from between the whore's legs, picking bits of fallopian tube from between his teeth.

The notorious pimp known as G-town Slim, knelt back down and continued chewing his way into the womb of his dying moneymaker. A universe of colors filled his head. He ate and ate until he could feel the power coursing through his blood stream. His father had been right. All along it had been right there. He had used it, abused, and sold it on street corners from Philadelphia to Las Vegas. But he'd never truly appreciated its power. Its glory. It had never occurred to him that pussy could be anything more than a receptacle for a man's seed. That it could possess the infinite power of eternity was something he'd never imagined. Either that or he was just high as hell.

G paused a second to take another hit of the cigar before kneeling back between Selena's blood-splattered thighs and tearing out her entire uterus with a sickening wet "Riiiiiip!" followed by a horrible slurping sound, as he swallowed her womanhood in a few quick gulps. Somewhere, within the darkened house, the other two girls were still screaming.

"Come on, son, we have to catch them," his father said. He could hear the girls pounding on his front door, trying to get out. One of them broke a window.

Still drunk off Opium, Xstasy, Absinthe, blood and pussy, G ignored his father and reached down to pick up Selena's discarded purse. He rummaged through it, withdrawing a handful of twenties.

"Two hundred fucking dollars? What the hell was that ho doing all night?!"

"Pimpin' ain't easy." His father snickered, shaking his head at his son's pitiful take.

The aging pimp's head looked once again like some carnivorous venus-flytrap vagina, with a razor-barbed clitoris and tusk-like fangs jutting forth from between the silken folds of flesh. G didn't find it so hideous anymore. He imagined he probably looked the same way now.

JOY

Again she drew the knife across her naked breasts, carving through her flesh and leaving long rivulets of blood crisscrossing her torso. Her arms, thighs, face, breasts, and stomach were crosshatched with slashes and cuts bleeding down her still staggeringly beautiful body. The cops surrounded her, pointing their guns and ordering her to drop the knife. That was one of the crowning moments of absurdity in a lifetime marked by madness and lunacy. If she didn't stop hurting herself the officers would shoot her.

The man upon whose flayed chest she knelt was Eddie Walker. He was a sadistic serial rapist and murderer who screamed and cried like the little girls he'd raped, when she disemboweled him. She wished she had the nerve to follow through with her threat to skip rope with his intestines. But she'd found the feel of his steaming, bloated entrails as repulsive as the smell. It smelled like vomit and ammonia.

Shana knew that God, her God, the God of her people, helped those who helped themselves. He gave you strength and the rest was up to you. She lifted the severed penis, still sizzling like a sausage on a grill, and the shriveled sack of burnt flesh where his testicles had been, up in front of her face and was surprised that she could not recognize it. It had only been ten years since she'd had it in her mouth. She spat at it and flipped it over her shoulder into the dirt, watching the cops wince and groan as they realized what it was that she was tossing at their feet.

Eddie moaned beneath her. Even with his torso bisected from his groin to the tip of his chin and his fat purple intestines boiling up out of the massive wound, he was still alive. Even with his genitals burnt to a blackened ruin, sawed off his body and scattered in different directions, he continued to breath. His heart continued to beat. It was true what they said. Evil never dies. Shana spit in his face.

It was not his fault alone that she had wound up this way. Her entire life had been marred by pain. She had never known joy.

Tears rolled down her face as she lifted her arms skyward and called out to the Lord. She knew it was futile. Hers was not a God of mercy. He didn't respond to self-pity. He didn't listen when her Nana cut out her clitoris with a sharp blade, no anesthesia, and sewed up her vagina with catgut to keep her pure for marriage and protect them all from the curse. He didn't hear her cry as her sex was mutilated ensuring that she would never enjoy sex as other women did. As she was prepared to become the property of her future husband once he'd purchased her for the price of thirty or forty cows, her virginity ensured by the destruction of her desire as was the custom in her culture. Even though she'd been born in America, and had never even been to Nigeria, and had been too young to understand that tradition had declared her sex fit only to be receptacles for a man's seed and nursemaid to his children. That a curse placed on her family centuries ago now placed a horrible penalty on anyone in her family who did not obey tradition.

She'd screamed and cried out for Chango, the Yuruba god of thunder and wrath, as her mother held her down and her Grandma took a thin blade used to filet fish to her most sensitive parts. Female circumcision they called it. It was supposed to keep her safe, protection against the family curse. She'd only been eight years old then. She'd been twelve when a filthy, wild-eyed, speed freak, who looked to her like the pictures she'd seen of Christ, had ripped wide the sutures on her labia. He cut through the stitches with a Swiss army knife before impaling her with his brutal penis, laughing at the thought that someone had tried so hard to keep him out, as he assaulted her in an alley she'd used as a short cut to school. Chango hadn't answered her prayers then either. Still, she'd called out his name over and over again as the man's sweat dripped from his brow into her eyes, his alcoholic breath steamed in her face, and his harsh and grimy hands pawed her young flesh while stabbing himself deep inside of her, ripping and tearing her tender flower.

Even then she'd somehow known that she was using his name in vain. Chango was the god of vengeance and wrath. He blessed his followers with the power to avenge injustice. It was up to them to survive it on their own.

Shana could remember looking in the mirror after she'd gotten home that day, looking at her smeared lipstick and torn clothes, the mascara running down her cheeks like black tears. Now she looked exactly like the whore her father had accused her of being when she first started wearing makeup. She knew then that no man would ever marry her now and her parents would blame it all on her. They'd always said that she'd become too wild and undisciplined, corrupted by the decadent American girls she played with. Funny that none of them had been punished as severely as she had. And all she'd done was put on lipstick and wake up too late to catch the school bus.

Storm clouds darkened the sky everyday after that. Sometimes a flash flood would pound the earth with a deluge of rain, washing away all the garbage from the streets and thunder would roar in the skies like the lion of Judah. Lightning bolts would strike the earth making it look like a battlefield, and Shana's parents would lock themselves in their rooms until it was over. Sometimes she would hear them whisper Chango's name in hushed reverent tones as the skies unleashed their fury and they cowered from his wrath. Other times they would whisper the name of "Obaluaiye" the god of pestilence, disease, and retribution. On those days, Shana would go out into the backyard and let the hard rain pound down over her. Hoping it would cleanse her of the memory of the assault, wash away his filth, which she could still feel on her skin like an oily film. Once the rain had continued for hours and the water level had risen to above her kneecaps. Still, she'd stood there adding her own tears to the rising torrent, as bolts of lightning scorched and churned the earth all around her.

Her parents had begun to look at her as if she had disgraced them, as if the rape had been her fault. Her father would threaten to emasculate the man with a dull knife when he finally caught up with the one responsible for violating his daughter's innocence and then in the very next breath accuse her of having none. Her mother and father would argue all the time about what to do with their "corrupted daughter" now that she'd been "ruined." Soon they seemed to lose all interest in finding the man who'd assaulted her. It had all been her fault.

They said she dressed too sexy and that's why she had been raped. So she stopped wearing skirts and shorts and only wore long pants and dresses and shirts that covered her arms so that none of her skin showed from her neck down. She stopped wearing makeup and cut her hair short. They said she was too friendly with boys. So she shunned them. They said her friends were a bad influence so she got rid of them too. They said her body developed too fast so she starved herself until her breasts and hips disappeared and her body looked like that of an adolescent boy. She listened to their arguments and would burst into tears when she heard her father call her a slut and accuse her of lying about the rape to cover up her promiscuity. Sometimes her mother would defend her and sometimes she wouldn't.

Every day that passed following the rape, her parents seemed to grow more agitated. There was a nervousness, a cautiousness, in the way they tip-toed around her. Despite the arguments they had with each other about her predicament, they hardly ever spoke to her about it. They hardly spoke to her at all anymore. She could sense them not wanting to be alone in the same room with her. They never looked her in the eyes or touched her anymore. It took a while for Shana to recognize their apprehension and hostility for what it was—fear. When her belly had begun to swell with pregnancy, their trepidation had turned to panic.

An endless procession of Yuruba priests and witchdoctor's began to attend to her almost daily. They prayed, meditated, and chanted over her and gave her herbs and medicines to drink. They gave her oils and ointments to rub over her belly. None of them would touch her. The rains would come almost immediately when they arrived and last for days after they left. The sky would rage, roaring out its pyrotechnic wrath and hurling a barrage of lightening bolts in every direction. Shana could see the terror on the faces of the priests increase as the dark clouds smothered the sky and the bolts of electricity struck closer and closer to her house. It was not uncommon for one to suddenly get up and flee the room. It was almost expected that the priests would fall ill soon after visiting her, and not even surprising when news of their deaths came back to the house. Shana had become a pariah, the shadow of death.

She never got to see her baby. She gave birth in her

bedroom surrounded by Yuruba priests and priestesses, candles, incense, and chalises to catch the blood of the offerings chained to her bedposts.

"We cannot just sacrifice a goat for this. Chango will want a greater offering." One wizened old priest said.

Her father lowered his head and pointed at Shana's belly.

"He shall have the child. That's what he wants."

"You can't! You can't do this!" her mother shrieked.

"We've tried everything else. There's nothing we can do!"

The earth shook as lightning scorched the earth all around their home. Smoke and car alarms went off all down the block. The louder Shana screamed with the throes of labor the more frequent and the closer the lightning struck. The priests and priestess began to slaughter the goats and chickens, slitting their throats and spraying their blood around the room. They danced and chanted and prayed. Then they began to shriek as the child came screaming from its mother's womb in a flood of blood of rage and the lightning smashed through the window knocking them to the floor and striking the bed.

Shana couldn't remember what happened after the room exploded with light and her head had filled with a sound like the earth itself cracking open. When she awoke, she was in the hospital and the baby was gone. No one ever told her what happened to it and she was forbidden to ask. The storms went away after that. However, her father's anger was even worse then before.

Just a few years later, mere days after Shana graduated from high school, her father kicked her out of the house. He refused to pay for her to go to college. He told her simply to "Pay her way the way the other whores did." So she'd started stripping. Her "exotic looks" had made her a favorite and soon she was being offered money to do more than take

28

off her clothes on stage. Soon she began to take it. Eddie had stolen all her pride and shame in that alley and her parents had made sure that she would never get it back. So what did it matter if she suffered another indignity or a hundred more? She was a slut now whether she took the money or not. So she'd begun to take their money, fucking without pleasure on sweaty motel mattresses and the cramped backseats of cars.

"Let me cum in your face, whore!"

"Take it up the ass, slut!"

"Come on and toss my salad for another hundred."

Shana had suffered every debasement imaginable. She'd sucked off two bikers in back of the club while another fucked her in the ass with a cock lubed only with saliva and another fisted her swollen vagina. They'd cheered when she began to cry and took turns jacking off in her open mouth before tossing her a measly hundred dollars, a fourth of what they'd promised her. She'd let a fat dyke who looked like Rosie O'Donnell with a mohawk savage her with a dildo the length and girth of a man's forearm while going down on the woman's morbidly obese life-partner who was easily twice as large, smothering beneath a mountain of gelatinous adipose tissue for a mere two-hundred dollars. Still, no matter how many times she shamed herself, no matter how much degradation and humiliation she put herself through, nothing erased the shame of that first time when she'd been innocent. Nothing erased the look in her father's eyes when she told him she'd been raped.

Then one day Eddie came into her club.

She recognized him right away, even though he'd grown a beard and looked now more like John the Baptist than Jesus Christ and more like Charlie Manson than either of them. She began to follow him, working up the courage to do something. Then, one day, he came to her and offered her money to drive with him into the park. She'd taken the money and her knife.

The storm clouds followed as they drove. Shana recognized them instantly. She knew they contained far more than rain. She felt a strength surge like fire within her. Her body felt charged with electricity. The hairs stood up all over her skin. Eddie was feeling it too. His hairs were standing up as well and the electrical system in his vehicle was going haywire. He turned off the stereo when the volume abruptly jumped to ten and the grunge rock turned to a static shriek of deafening white noise.

Shana's nerves were jangling like live wires and a rage was building inside her, a wrath so powerful it felt like an alien presence within her. They left the car and walked into the park. James immediately began to paw at her, raising his hand to strike her when she resisted. Shana obeyed, allowing him to force her head down into his lap, taking his sweaty cock down her throat and ignoring the tart tangy taste of smegma and the syphilitic drip from the tip off his cock. She listened to him moan and shout obscenities at her as he forced his cock further and further into her throat until her nose was buried in the musty stench of his unwashed pubic-hair. She let her rage build as he gripped the back of her head and thrust even deeper as he came in a thick hot gout of semen that splashed the back of her throat and made her wretch. Then he pulled his still erect cock out of her mouth and squeezed the last drops of his seed onto her face where they dribbled down her cheeks like tears of pearl. The fury in her eyes went completely unnoticed.

"Yeah, bitch. That was perfect. You suck that dick like you were born to it. But you know what I really want. I want to fuck you in that fat ass of yours. I love how you nigger bitches have those big round asses. Bend over bitch!"

That was the word. The same word he had used when

he raped her the first time years ago. It was the word women like her had heard from the lips of white slave masters since this sinful country was born. It was the word of violence, and hatred, and oppression, and rape. It was the last time she'd ever tolerate it. It would be the last words Eddie would ever speak.

Shana's thick wooly hair filled with sparks and her eyes roiled with blue-white fury like ball lightning as she seized Eddie's nutsack with both hands and dug her nails into them. Searing heat blazed through his testicles churning his guts in agony as Shana twisted his balls in hands that coursed with electricity. His testes sizzled, boiling in her hands as Eddie's screams reached a falsetto she would have never guessed him capable of. They popped like suppurating pimples, exploded in her fingers like eggs in a microwave, spraying whatever semen remained within them out onto the grass. His nutsack caught fire turning Eddie's pubic hair into a burning bush as his genitals were charred to a cinder. He opened his mouth to scream before the lightning left her and threw him twenty feet back.

Rippling waves of energy surrounded Shana as she approached Eddie with the ire of a God within her, filling the hollow spot where the child she'd carried for nine months had nestled. He cringed helplessly in the dirt, clutching his blackened genitals, as the rain began to fall and lightning pounded the earth. He could hear it getting closer and closer until it was right on top of him, striking him repeatedly, tossing him about like a leaf in a dust storm.

The electricity fried his brain in his skull. By the time the police followed the source of the unearthly cries of anguish to their source, the skies had cleared and Shana had already begun to take her own anger out on the near vegetable laying in the mud at her feet. She was still cutting on him when they leapt from their cars with weapons drawn. Then she'd begun cutting herself.

It had been her Great grandmother's beauty that had first drawn a God from the heavens to mate with her and it was Shana's beauty that had drawn Eddie. So now she meant to destroy that beauty and forever escape both of their attentions.

Eddie could no longer control his own motorfunctions. The necessary synapses in his nervous system had been fried. He could not remember who he was or why he was in pain. Why the woman with the flaming eyes was hurting him, cutting and ripping at him. Why she was cutting herself. He could see the pain in her eyes and some dim part of his brain told him that he was responsible, that he deserved this, and that it was going to get worse. That it had to get worse before he could be forgiven. If he could ever be forgiven.

He knew that he'd already been badly wounded, perhaps even fatally. He looked at his ruined and ransacked torso and wondered how he was even conscious with so much damage done to him. So much pain.

"Forgive me," he begged. But she couldn't hear him. Because his lips and tongue were no longer responding to his commands. They would not move to make the sounds. He tried again and only managed to make bubbles of saliva. He looked up into her eyes. The flame was gone and she was back to being a hurt and angry little girl. A very angry little girl. But something in those dark jewels told him that she would forgive him if he could only form the words. He bubbled up more saliva and watched as she raised the knife above her. Her eyes began to roil and flame again. A long wail escaped Eddie's mouth and tears rolled down his face.

He remembered what he had done now. Though he couldn't remember this woman specifically, he remembered the faces of the little girls he had attacked, any one of which could have been her or her child. He could hear the echo of their screams fill the dark voids in his memory and he knew then that he would not be forgiven by this woman. He knew that he should not be forgiven.

Eddie looked up at the clouds assembling overhead, dark angry clouds, and saw faces forming within them with furious eyes just like the woman with the knife. He saw the face of a sorrowful child who looked just like him. They scowled down at him shrieking with rage in voices of thunder. Their faces widened and split apart as their roars shook the earth and lightning spilled from their eyes, screaming for his blood. He cowered in the mud wondering which would kill him first; the angry gods roiling in the dark nimbus above him or the mad woman aiming the knife down at his face.

"This is your last warning! Put the knife down and back away from that man! Put it down now!"

The police yelled at her waving their guns and Shana smiled. She could see the storm clouds moving back in, she could feel the energy rising within her, and she took back all she'd said about God never helping her. God, her God, had heard her and he was coming.

Lightning rained down its fiery wrath upon the earth and Shana smiled and laughed as the rain washed over her, healing her wounds. She thrust the knife into Eddie's eyesocket and heard him gurgle his last living words before hell took his soul. Bolts of electricity smashed the cop cars like toys and reduced the officers to panicked screams. Shana watched as all the pain and horror of her life erupted forth in bolts of electric fire, burning her tormentors to shrieking cinders and for the first time, since her mother held her down while her Nana mutilated her, she knew real joy.

KIDS

Jeff had no one to blame but himself. He hugged her and the chill from her flesh raised goose bumps all over his arms. She stared at him as if he was the biggest fool on earth. A character assessment he couldn't contest. Her lips were set in a hard line that discouraged kisses. Jeff knew that, under different circumstances, she would have spit in his face or at least stormed out of the house in annoyance and disgust.

Her cold eyes passed judgment on his manhood and once again Jeff felt humiliated. A Failure. Impotent. Not a real man. All the words that had caused him to strangle her in the first place. When his erection had dwindled and her scornful laughter and harsh words scalded his ego like an acid bath, killing her had made him feel powerful again. Potent and virile. As her pulse rate dwindled beneath the crushing pressure of his murderous hands, his erection had come surging back. Its solid length giving him confidence that this time he would be able to consummate their love.

"It's these damned condoms!" he shrieked. "I can't feel a fucking thing through these goddamn sensory deprivation jackets! They cut off my fucking circulation!" He ripped his revitalized erection free of its latex sheath, tossing the shredded pieces of rubber to the floor.

At his wife's insistence, Jeff had waited until his marriage day to even see her naked. She wasn't exactly a virgin. She'd had a string of lesbian lovers before she'd turned hetero who'd penetrated her with dildos the size of baseball bats, but he was the first real man she'd ever been with or at least, that's what she'd told him. He often wondered. Sometimes he felt she resented him for making her fall in love with him and then falling short of her idealized fantasies of manhood. After all, his six inches was no comparison to the eleven-inch vibrating monstrosity she still kept in a suitcase in her closet.

On their honeymoon, she had enthusiastically wrestled his turgid flesh into a cocoon of spermicidal latex then injected herself with foam and lay back with her legs spread wide to receive him. Jeff's erection had fainted dead away as if shocked by a taser-gun. Every night since had been some replay of the same. He'd learned to fall asleep to the whirr of the vibrator echoing from deep within her.

"If you'd have only let me do it without this thing on this wouldn't have happened!"

Jeff looked down at his wife who lay there turning blue, her tongue lolling out of her mouth like a fat slug, turning purple, her eyes rolled up in her head, urine and spermicidal jelly leaking from her slack vagina. It was still stretched out from its many nights with the King Kong vibrator that substituted for him when he was unable to perform. He tore open her legs aggressively, nearly disjointing her hips in his enthusiasm. Taking his hardening sex in hand, he entered her lifeless husk and made love to her for the first time. All the pressure and performance anxiety gone. No expectations to live up to. No past lovers to compete with. No frustrated looks of disappointment to contend with. Two strokes in he knew she'd been right about him all along.

She was wetter than he ever could have imagined and her vagina was a miracle of muscular development. It wasn't just the body fluids evacuating her corpse or the involuntary contraction of her powerful kegel muscles as she spasmed in her death throes. It felt as if there were tongues inside of her, slurping on the tip of his tumescent cock. The sensation was overwhelming. Every muscle in his body locked and began to convulse violently as the orgasm erupted from him in a white molten torrent of shame. Premature ejaculation. Whatever it was wriggling and writhing within her (and Jeff was sure he didn't want to speculate) it had quickly and efficiently milked him of his seed. Even dead she was too much woman for him.

"My god! What the hell was that?"

The death rictus on her face looked to him now like a mocking smile. Jeff withdrew his spent and shriveled organ from her lukewarm flesh and turned his head away from her eyes, which he could feel burning into his skull. Cold. Accusatory.

"Fuck you! I'm a man! I'm a man, you heartless bitch! You just make me so nervous staring at me like that!"

But she's dead. Why should it matter how she looks at me? Jeff wondered.

He reached out and closed her eyes. Now, she didn't look so intimidating. She looked kind of pleasant except for that pained grin. Jeff tried to pull her lips down over her teeth, but wasn't sure just how to do that. He tugged on them until he was afraid he would rip them off. Then he decided to pry her mouth open instead. He reached under the bed for his shoehorn and wedged it in between her teeth. With just the slightest bit of effort he was able to open her mouth. It was a mistake. She wasn't snickering and grinning anymore. Now she was laughing boisterously.

"Shut the fuck up! Shut up!" He yelled.

He drew his hand back and slapped her across the face again and again, but her laughter continued.

36

"I'll shut your ass the fuck up."

He took himself in hand and leaned over her, jamming his limp penis into her mouth. She hadn't given him a blowjob since the day he said, "I do". But now she was in no position to refuse.

"Who's laughing now, bitch? Huh? Who's laughing now?"

The feel of her tepid saliva on the head of his manhood put the steel back in his erection. He began slowly fucking her face, ramming his stiffening cock down her throat. The idea of cumming in her mouth caused his organ to swell larger than it had in years. He could feel it throbbing deep in her esophagus as he raped her throat, thrusting harder and faster. He could feel the orgasm building, that familiar tingling sensation roiling at the base of his cock, but he withdrew, breathing deeply to get himself back under control. There was something else he wanted to try even more.

Jeff rolled his wife over onto her belly and slathered his thumb in saliva then inserted it into his wife's anus. She would have never even considered allowing him this type of pleasure when she was alive. She would have filed for divorce at the mere suggestion of anal sex, but since he was probably headed for death row anyway, he might as well have as much fun with her as he could before she began to rot and her stench brought nosy neighbors and cops.

He pushed his penis deep into the slippery wetness of her sphincter, lubricated with the blood and excrement leaking sluggishly from her relaxed bowels, and was rewarded with that same sensation of tongues slithering over his cock. Then he began to scream as something clamped down hard on his penis and began to rip and tear at it. Quickly he withdrew his cock with a wet sticky "Schlorp!" as he fell out of his wife's corpse and onto the floor, screeching like a cat on fire.

Jeff looked down in horror at his vandalized manhood and

found it a bloody ruin. He stared closer as he whimpered in pain and saw little teeth marks on his penis where something had bitten chunks out of the rapidly diminishing organ. Jeff looked across the floor and began to scream again when he saw what was wriggling free of his dead wife's asshole.

Terror creeped slowly up his spine, raising the hairs on the back of his neck as he watched a nest of blind hairless things come boiling up out of her anus, eating away at her buttocks as they struggled to free themselves. Pale, slimy, larval creatures, with piranha-like teeth and human faces, a nauseating hybrid of maggot and fetus, worming their way out of her intestinal track by way of her dilated rectum, gnashing their teeth and greedily chomping on glistening red strips of intestinal and hemorrhoidal tissue. Their pinched and wrinkled faces looked like some combination of Jeff and his wife.

Is this what our children would have looked like? He wondered in disgust. *No wonder she never let me fuck her without a condom.*

He'd long known that his wife Lucretia wasn't exactly of this earth. He'd met her in a graveyard at midnight on Christmas Eve. He'd gone there to steal a fresh corpse for his yearly Winter Solstice Necromancing ritual. The recently interred body of a local Catholic Bishop who'd been castrated and shot dead by the father of an alter boy he'd been molesting. There was strong magic in the corpses of disgraced religious leaders. But when he'd pried open the crypt he'd found Lucretia there with half the bishop's heart and brains already digesting in her stomach and the remains still being stuffed into her slavering mouth. It had been love at first sight.

She was naked and her breasts were full and round with large inch long nipples, pale and smooth like new snow. Her body was a wet dream of voluptuous curves, flawless cream-colored skin, and eyes the color of liquid night shining in the moonlight. The sight of the blood and gore drooling off her chin, dripping down her neck and between her cleavage, transfixed him. She was inhumanly beautiful. He'd dropped to his knees in worship before her and he'd been her slave ever since, just like any good marriage. Only there's had been practically sexless. Mostly due to his own deficiencies and Lucretia's peculiar safe sex fetish.

As the product of his sperm and her accursed ovum slithered out of his wife's bowels, trailing feces and blood, Jeff thought of an old joke he'd heard once from some comedian whose name he couldn't recall.

"Don't wear a condom and you can catch something worse than AIDS...like KIDS!"

The creatures began consuming Lucretia's corpse. Jeff tried to crawl away, but soon they were swarming all over him as well, voraciously gnawing at his flesh as he cried out in anguish. They wriggled beneath his skin, devouring all the subcutaneous muscle and fat and burrowing deeper into his organs. He punched and kicked trying to fight them off, punching himself in the stomach in an attempt to crush the ones already inside him. A wave of nausea rolled over him as he watched his belly undulate, filled with the fruit of his loins.

Jeff's eyes rolled up in his head, the pain overwhelming, as he felt something crunch down on his heart. In his periphery vision he saw the remains of the condom he'd torn to shreds. In the morning the police would find it laying beside his corpse like a safe sex advertisement and they would chuckle at the irony, just as Jeff himself did, seconds before his heart went down the gullet of his offspring.

FEEDING TIME

Sandy watched the sinuous, hyper-muscular black man slide open the little trapdoor to the lion's habitat. Her breath seized in her chest as he began to chuck in large slabs of thick, dripping, arterial red meat. The lions responded, eagerly pouncing on the meal and shredding into it with ravenous enthusiasm. Seeing the tremendous power in their slavering jaws as they ripped and tore at the raw and bloody chunks of flesh turned Sandy on more than anything else she could imagine. Her arousal dripped down her inner thigh and scented the air with a sweet sticky musk filled with female pheromones.

Watching the big cats always did that to her. Their sleek and elegant power, their savage strength, their tremendous fangs and claws, and equally impressive cocks. There was something alluring about a creature that beautiful and that dangerous.

Getting fucked by one of the huge jungle cats had been a fantasy of Sandy's ever since she was a little girl. She'd never fantasized about anything else since the day she'd first learned to masturbate. Why waste time trying to find a man who was a lion in the bedroom when you could go straight to the king of the jungle himself? She'd tried the peanut butter on the clitoris trick with the household cat but it wasn't quite the same. Although the kitten's soft fur and rough tongue had excited her as it whispered between her thighs, they weren't resilient enough to withstand her urgent thrusting and she'd broken more than one kitten's neck thrusting her pelvis against it before giving up on the experiment. She needed something bigger, stronger, meaner.

Watching them rend and mutilate the chunks of raw cow flesh, slashing it to a strawberry red pulp, made her nipples harden and rub against the satin lining of her chinchilla coat. Seeing their murderous fangs wet with blood made her clitoris swell in anticipation and her labia drip with beads of moisture. Imagining that those chunks were pieces of her scumbag husband's corpse turned her on even more. Sandy's legs went weak. She squirmed with a mounting arousal as she sat on the bench watching the ferocious beasts scarf down their blood drenched meal.

Two of the large cats began fighting over a particularly fat hunk of bleeding flesh. Unable to control her excitement, Sandy reached under her coat and slid a dildo up into her now dripping wet snatch. The savagery of their feeding frenzy made her so horny she didn't care who saw her.

She was naked beneath her long coat and she pounded the eight-inch rubber cock up inside herself while vigorously rubbing her engorged clitoris. Two of the larger cats roared and slashed at each other and Sandy imagined that the huge beasts were gang raping her. Biting the back of her neck as they thrust their huge hairy cocks into her sore, wet little pussy, into her ass, down her throat. She imagined that she was being fucked by the two lions as the rest of the pride ripped her husband's corpse to a bright red ruin. She imagined taking one of their massive organs down her throat, hearing him let out a roar that shook the earth as an orgasm ripped through him and his cum flooded her mouth. She fucked herself with the dildo faster and faster building to a frantic orgasm as the lions savagely consumed their meal, fingering her swollen clit as she envisioned herself gagging on bucket loads of lion semen. Sandy imagined watching her husband scream as they mauled and tore at his salon-tanned, Bowflex-muscled torso. His steaming viscera flayed open with their savage claws.

Lost in ecstasy, she licked her lips in unison with the monstrous felines as they lapped thick meaty blood from their whiskers. She spread her legs wide and fucked herself hard with the big plastic dick, not caring who saw her, giving the zoo handler a perfect view of her lovely pussy. He had seen her there before, though never so blatant as today. He'd noticed her lustful stares into the cage as he approached with the meat. At first he thought she was just hungry, jealous that he would waste such good meat on the cats when she needed a meal. Then he thought she wanted him. It wasn't until today that he realized that it was the cats themselves that she wanted. It wasn't until today that he noticed that she'd been fingering herself all along.

Seeing her fuck herself with the synthetic cock, he found himself hopelessly aroused. He took off his latex glove and dipped his hand into the bucket of blood and flesh. With his other hand he unleashed the tremendous black trouser snake from his zipper. He lubed up his swollen cock with the fistful of blood and began stroking himself while he watched Sandy and she watched the cats. Sandy noticed him just before she started to cum and their eyes locked as he shot a load of hot white semen into the bucket of raw flesh and she slid the entire dildo up inside herself and shook with an orgasm that tore through her like electricity. It was so early in the morning that neither of them were spotted except by the old lady who came to feed the flamingos and she was too crazy and senile to care. It probably gave her a thrill.

Sandy withdrew the long dildo from her silken folds and brought it to her lips, still staring at the zoo handler who still had his cock in his hand on the other side of the lion's cage.

She stared at the man's massive organ. Its head still glistened with semen and blood and it was at least still partially erect. Even at half-mast it was bigger than her little sex toy. She imagined fucking the huge black man against the lion's cage and began getting aroused all over again. She slid the dildo into her mouth, sucking and licking her own juices from it.

The zoo attendant's cock began to stiffen again and he once more began to stroke himself with a fist lubed with cow's blood. Sandy rose from the bench and began walking over to the door just beyond the lion's habitat, which read "Zoo Employees Only" and "Dangerous Animals. Do Not Enter." She was still sucking on the dildo when he opened the door for her and he was still stroking his magnificent cock.

Sandy slipped inside the dark corridor and fell into the zoo attendant's incredible arms. Feeling the power in his huge biceps and forearms, the hardness of his rippling pecs, the stiffness of his cock, she was immediately reminded of the lions. He kissed her deeply, tasting the juices of her sex on her tongue. Then she took his throbbing organ in her hand and led him down the hall and back to the lion's cage.

Positioning him so that she could watch the lion's while enjoying him, she knelt down and took his cum and blood encrusted organ down her throat, gagging as it hit her tonsils, but still guiding it further until it filled her throat. She watched the lions purring contentedly with their bellies filled with domestic beef as she gorged herself on her own brand of grade-A prime beef. She still had the dildo in her hand and was pumping it in and out of her juicy wet cunt as she sucked off the massive black man with the bloody hands.

The zoo attendant stepped out of his pants and removed his shirt. His body was all thick, hard, striated muscles crosshatched with throbbing veins. He looked almost as ferocious and powerful as the lions. His eyes blazed with a lust as fearsome as the predators' appetite. He turned Sandy around onto all fours and reached his hand back into the bucket of blood, once again lubing up his enormous cock. Using the cow's blood as lubricant he eased his dick into her puckered rose-colored asshole. Sandy squealed, the zoo attendant roared, and they both began to moan and purr in unison as their pleasure spiraled. Enraptured by their violent passion the lions charged the cage, snarling and purring and rubbing their bodies against the iron bars. With her asshole filled with nearly ten inches of black cock, Sandy reached into the bucket and pulled out the last piece of bloody meat, now slick with semen, and began cramming it into her mouth, greedily gnawing at it, relishing the copper flavor of blood and the salty taste of fresh semen. She passed what was left of the meat through the bars where it was snatched up by one of the ravenous jungle cats. She felt her clitoris swell as she scratched at it with her fingernails, felt her kegel muscles contract around the dildo, and her sphincter muscles lock tight on the zoo attendant's enormous dick. By the time she felt the boiling hot explosion of cum erupting into her ass, her own orgasm followed it in a jerking, flailing, thrashing, fury.

Sandy arrived home that night and was not surprised to hear the wet burping sound of her husband getting his asshole stretched by the neighbor's oversized cock. She had thought she could change him. She'd believed him when he told her he loved her and wanted to go straight. She'd even tried to accommodate his lusts, to act as a surrogate for the donkey-dicked gigolos and prostitutes he ordered over the internet. She'd purchased massive dildos and strap-ons in an effort to try to give him the pleasure he found in other men. He swore to her that he had given up men and that he would be a faithful husband. Then she'd come home early one night to find him laughing in the arms of their next door neighbor, Big Hank, a thick, hairy, biker-looking, ex-Rock & Roll star with a dick nearly as big as the Mandingo zoo attendant whose cum she could still taste on her tongue. She'd listened to him tell Big Hank about how he'd just used her to get his inheritance. How it had been a condition of his father's will that he marry a woman before he could get the million and a half bequeathed to him when his millionaire father drowned in the pool after one too many martinis. So he'd talked her into believing that he could give up dick for pussy.

"This guy comes up to me at the coffee shop down the street and just asks me out of nowhere if I'm gay. I look him up and down and said, 'Let me put it to you this way. I don't eat pussy and I don't like foreplay.' You should have seen his jaw drop. Fucking breeders are such idiots. Like I could really enjoy eating pussy when you're lying next door with that big fat dick all thick and juicy. Sandy asked me to go down on her the other night and I almost threw up all over her. Hell, I don't even like sushi! I only married the silly bitch to get my inheritance."

That first night, as she watched from the shadows, mortified as her husband Bruce took Hank's fat cock down his throat, slurping and gulping until what looked like a full pint of cum exploded from the man's cock into Bruce's face, she knew she had to get back at him. She watched him lick semen from his lips, wiping it from his cheeks, chin, from where it had dribbled down his neck and between his sculptured pecs with the back of his hand, before licking his fingers clean. She sat silently, weeping in the next room as he bent Hank over and fucked that fat bastard in his big hairy ass more passionately than he had ever fucked her. And she knew that he was right. She would never be able to please him. But she wouldn't be a fool either. She wouldn't let herself be treated like an idiot by anyone.

It was soon after that that she'd begun going back down to the lion cages. She hadn't been there since she was in high school. Back before she'd ever had sex. When fingering herself while the big cats tore slabs of meat to shreds was all the sexual fulfillment she'd ever needed. She'd gone back to the cages only to find that now her desire was so much larger than it had been as an adolescent. Her fantasies now involved pain and death and vengeance. She wanted to see her husband in that cage and she wanted to be in there with him. Fucking Bruce's conquerors. Licking his blood from their whiskers. Feeling their rough tongues on her swollen clitoris. Taking their hairy cocks down her throat while Bruce's blood washed over her. And now she had the means to do it.

She watched a while longer as Hank punched his cock lubed with Astro Glide and saliva up into Bruce's colon. Bruce moaned as the thick organ pounded in and out of his dilated rectum and Hank's fat meaty hand reached around to stroke her husband to orgasm. Even in the violence of their lovemaking there was an intimacy that had never been there when she and Bruce had fumbled their way toward orgasm. Between them, lovemaking had always been stale and mechanical. They would both think about anything but each other as they masturbated within each other's flesh. No passion, just the release of biological fluids as artless and automatic as urination. She wept silently, even as she began fingering herself again. For the first time in their marriage, in separate rooms, she and her husband reached orgasm at the same time.

Sandy had been fucking her beautiful Mandingo zoo attendant for nearly a month, coming home reeking of cow's blood and semen without Bruce even appearing to notice. They were growing more estranged. No more pathetic attempts to mimic homosexual lovemaking. Now the dildos and vibrators were strictly for her lunch time zoo excursions.

Bruce was getting even more flagrant with his affair. She

would find condoms and empty vials of lubricant under the couch. She would often pass Hank coming out of the front door as she entered into a home that stank of cum, Astro Glide and ass. She even sat through an entire dinner, staring at the dried semen in Bruce's goatee without saying a word. She kissed him good night, tasting Hank's cum on his lips.

The last straw was when she came home to find him with his face pressed between Hank's fat hairy buttocks and his tongue halfway up the fat rocker's ass. Her stomach rolled with revulsion as she watched him ream the rotund has-been Rock & Roller while jacking him off. Just before he came, Hank turned around so he could shoot his load onto Bruce's outstretched tongue. Bruce lapped up Hank's salty semen as it rained down onto his face. Sandy stormed out of the house.

That night, Sandy came home and Bruce tried to pretend as if nothing had happened. He even tried to kiss her with the scent and taste of Hank's rectum still on his breath and Hank's cum once again drying in his moustache. That's when Sandy finally snapped. She stormed out of the room, down to the basement to retrieve a hammer from the tool rack. When she returned, Bruce was already in the shower washing off his lover's sweat and semen. He stepped out of the shower with welts and hickeys on his ass cheeks along with the obvious impression of a very large hand and Sandy struck him over the head with the hammer. She hit him again and again until she was certain he wouldn't get up again. He lay on the bathroom floor bleeding, moaning, and convulsing. She knew he'd be dead soon, but hopefully not too soon.

"You've got to help me. I need you to open up the zoo for me. Open up the lion's cage."

"For what? It's after midnight!"

"I know, but I need your help. I just killed my husband." Sandy said.

"You what?"

"I killed Bruce."

"Oh, you must be sick if you think I'm getting involved in that shit!"

"Listen, Bruce was a millionaire and all his money will go to me if he dies and I don't get convicted. At any rate I still have access to all his accounts. I could bring you fifty thousand dollars tonight. He keeps at least that much in our safe. You've got to help me. Pleeease?"

"Fifty thousand?"

"I can bring it to you right now if you'll help me."

There was hardly a pause. Money was indeed, the root of all evil. Money and pride.

"Okay, I'll do it. But why don't we just bury him? Why the lion's cage?"

"You know why," Sandy replied coyly in a low sultry voice. "I'll give you another fifty-thousand when it's all over. Just let me have my fantasy."

Sandy watched as her magnificent ebon lover hefted her husband out of the trunk, his titanic muscles straining under her husband's dead weight. She let out a little squeal when Bruce began to groan and he dropped him hard onto the concrete.

"Shit! I thought you said he was dead?"

"What does it matter? I gave you your money. He'll be dead soon."

"I don't know about this."

"Don't you want me to suck that beautiful cock of yours? Swallow all that delicious cum? Bring you all that pretty money? Well I want this!"

"Okay, but I think we're going to need to renegotiate."

"Will another fifty-thousand make up your mind for you? I'll let you fuck me in the ass just like you like."

She reached out and began to stroke his massive cock

through his pants and that decided the matter for him. He threw Bruce's semi-conscious body over his shoulders like it was a sack of laundry and jogged from the parking lot to the rear zoo gate, not even needing to put him down while he fished his keys out of his pocket and let himself in. He wasn't even breathing hard.

They crept past the reptile habitat, past the monkey cage, the otters, and the giraffes, before a heavy roar announced their arrival at the lions cage.

"Dump him in! Throw his ass in there!" Sandy ordered excitedly, already stripping out of her clothes. The zoo attendant walked over and opened the side door, carrying Bruce into the hallway and back to the rear of the cage. The lions could smell the blood leaking from the wound in Bruce's scalp. They immediately began to crowd against the bars of the cage.

When Bruce's body finally squeezed through the trap door into the cage the lions immediately began to fight over his flesh, snarling savagely as they tore off the choice pieces of meat. Deliriously horny, Sandy tore off the zoo attendant's shorts and began swallowing his dick. Naturally, she'd brought along her dildo and was furiously fucking herself with it as she sucked him off, staring into the cage as the huge alpha male fought back the other lions and turned toward Bruce, who was now conscious, grievously injured, and screaming his lungs out. Sandy took that massive cock all the way down her throat while swirling her tongue around the tip. Her eyes teared up as she fought the gag reflex, allowing the thick foot long member further into her gullet while he dug his fingers into her hair and thrust even deeper, raping her esophagus. Sandy, gagging on the massive dick and loving every minute of it, tickled his balls with her long manicured nails and slipped a finger into his anus to massage his prostate, causing her lover to immediately cum in a molten torrent. Warm semen filled her mouth, spilling out over her chin and down over her lovely breasts as the fearsome cat ripped open her husband's stomach and began tearing out and consuming his organs with his terrible blood-soaked fangs.

"Oh God! Sandy! Help me! Help meeeeeeee!" Bruce screamed, beating at the terrifying beasts with his feeble fists, his strength bleeding out onto the hard concrete floor of the cage.

Her eyes went cold and ruthless as she watched her husband's agony, still licking cum from her lips and from her lover's cock then hot with passion as the sight of him being mauled by the pride of hungry lions further excited her. Sandy was in a frenzy of voluptuous rapture, her arousal rising in proportion to the lion's bloodlust and, as usual, her beautiful obsidian stallion was still hard. He turned her around and slammed his tremendous organ into her ass, mercilessly fucking her tight anus.

"Oh yes! Yes! Fuck me harder! Harder!" Sandy went wild watching her husband scream and beg while the lions tore him apart and her lover ravaged her asshole.

"Oh God! Help! Noooooo! Arrrrrrrrgh!"

The lion tore out her Bruce's throat and Sandy came, screaming, crying, hissing and cussing, as her lover filled her ass with his seed. A bright red arterial spray splashed across her face and Sandy came again as the lion cracked open her husband's ribcage and savagely ripped out his heart.

She fell back onto the hard floor, panting breathlessly as her beautiful black Adonis withdrew his spent organ from her ass.

"You don't love me do you?" he asked.

"What? What the fuck are you talking about?" Sandy asked still winded from her orgasm.

"You don't even know my fucking name, but yet you

want me to share a murder rap with you? No way sister."

"I know your name. You're uh... um... Terrance?"

"Terrell! We've been fucking for almost a month and you don't know shit about me!"

"What the fuck does it matter anyway?"

He grabbed her by her wrists, pinning both her arms together in one huge hand, and dragged her over to the feeding door.

"It matters to me," he said. "See, there's no statute of limitations on murder. A crazy bitch like you might suddenly get an attack of conscience and confess then I go down as an accessory to murder."

"Why would I tell anyone? We're in this together!"

"Yeah, but you're a rich white woman and I'm just some broke-ass nigga. You could blame all of this shit on me and skate Scott free. There's only one way that two people can keep a secret like this and that's if one of them is dead."

Sandy's eye's bulged in horror as she stared into the cage where the ravenous cats were busy working her husband's flesh free from his bones. She began to fight and struggle, but Terrell was impossibly, hopelessly strong. He easily subdued her and the struggle caught the attention of the lions. Sandy trembled in horror as the lions crowded against the cage, licking their gore-streaked fangs; bits of blood, flesh, and sinew, still clinging to their fur.

Despite her terror, Sandy felt a tremor of excitement between her thighs and a salacious wetness at the prospect of being at the mercy of those beautiful, powerful, ravenous beasts. She began fucking herself with the dildo again. Terrell looked down as he heard her begin to moan and pant.

"You are fucking unbelievable!" He said as he watched her masturbate to her own imminent death. And with that he opened up the door and threw her into the cage.

Sandy screamed. This was nothing like her fantasy. Sandy

spread her legs to offer her luscious pussy to her magnificent feline lovers and at first they licked obediently. She moaned and cooed, delirious with pleasure. Then they began to bite, tearing through her labia up into her ovaries. Sandy offered them her full round breasts and they slashed them with their claws. Ripping off her nipples and consuming her luscious mammaries.

Knowing this would be her dying act, her last chance to live out her fantasy, she reached out for the alpha male's cock and began to suck him off. Sandy took his entire length down her throat even as the voracious cat burrowed his snout into her belly to consume her organs in a gruesome parody of a "69." A roar split the night air as the big cat shuddered with a violent orgasm, filling her throat with lion semen and choking off her screams, even as he tore out Sandy's liver.

Terrell took himself in hand and began stroking himself towards another orgasm as he watched his beautiful lover fulfill her fantasy.

ROTTWEILER

Joey squeezed his eyes shut and concentrated hard. He was sick of being hurt, sick of being afraid. He had never been afraid when his dad was still around. He'd always felt safe wrapped in his father's enormous arms. But now, it felt like he was always terrified, always being victimized, by the bullies at school, the bigger kids in the neighborhood, and, worst of all, the sitter.

Joey's mother had bought him a dog after his father had left them to keep the house safe while they slept. A big Rottweiler named Hades who'd been Shutzhund trained at the same academy where they trained the police canine units.

"Who needs a man," she'd said, "We've got Hades to look after us. She's like a burglar alarm that bites!"

But Joey was the only one who needed protecting.

"Joeey? Joooooeeeeey?"

Her voice was malevolently sweet like Halloween candy filled with razors. Prickles of fear dashed the length of Joey's spine raising goosebumps on the back of his neck and causing his scrotum to shrink up tight against him. An involuntary whimper escaped his throat and his knees began to shake. He could smell his own fear, an acrid musk like sweat and urine that made his eyes water and glued his tongue to the roof of his mouth. He was ashamed of his fear. Tears wept from the corners of his eyes and he wiped them away with the sleeve of his pajamas. He was determined to be strong.

Joey tried to tell himself that he had nothing to be afraid of. He had Hades there to protect him. But she was locked up downstairs in her kennel and he was upstairs. Alone. And the bad woman was getting closer. He could hear her.

"Joooey? Where are you little Joey?"

He tried to ignore that repulsive sing song voice. To shut out the sound of her stealthy footsteps creeping towards him down the hall, to steady his breathing, clear his mind, and reach out for Hades, downstairs in her kennel.

Joey had asked his mother to leave Hades in his room so she could watch over him. But the babysitter insisted the dog be locked up. Now he could hear the fat, perverted sitter getting closer to his door. He knew she'd be coming in soon—to touch him. Joey quieted his thoughts and washed his mind clear.

"Help me, Hades."

The huge Rottweiler sat locked in a cage downstairs in his father's old den. Joey could feel her rage boiling up through the floorboards; feel it filling him, giving him strength. He could feel her breath, her heartbeat. He could taste the dog food stuck between her teeth; feel the long ropes of saliva drooling from the corners of her mouth. He could even feel the tick behind her left ear. Joey's heartbeat sped up and fell in sync with the powerful metronome thundering in the big dog's chest. His breathing grew deeper, huskier. A growl rumbled low in his throat.

Joey let himself slip away. He concentrated on his monstrous pet until everything else disappeared. Until he felt their consciousnesses merge. Joey's bedroom doorknob turned. The babysitter was coming.

"Where are you Joeeeey?"

Hades went wild. Savage growls and barks echoed from down in the den. She wanted to protect him, to keep the bad woman from hurting him. Joey knew the big dog would've torn the babysitter apart if she could, if she weren't imprisoned. The dog's thoughts filled his head with images of ripping flesh, crunching bone, severed arteries and ligaments. The dog's muscles tensed, her massive jaws clenched as her lips pulled away from her fangs and her snout wrinkled into a snarl. She lowered her head toward the floor with her ears flattened back against her skull and paws splayed out in front of her, preparing to launch forward and pounce on her prey. The doorknob continued to turn.

"Help me. Help me. Help me."

The growls and snarls grew louder.

"Shut the fuck up, you stupid dog!"

The babysitter's voice was so close now. The door opened and the obese woman shambled in with the light from the hallway silhouetting her massive form. Her balloon-like breasts were perched atop a leather corset, squashing her bloated mammary glands up around her neck. She wore a leather harness around her waist that wrapped up between her titanic cellulite smothered thighs and held a lethal looking plastic phallus.

"It's playtime, Joey."

The babysitter grinned lasciviously as she waddled towards the bed with her artificial penis slapping one thigh then the other. But her smile fell hard and shattered into a scream when she spotted the big dog snarling at her from Joey's bed. Eyes catching moonlight and twirling it around its retinas like a kaleidoscope beneath a brow furrowed with rage. Muscles bunched up beneath its fur. Saliva dripping from long curved fangs glowing luminescent in the scant light. The huge Rottweiler sprang from Joey's bed and locked its jaws on her throat.

Joey wasn't afraid any more. He was ferocious as he tore into his tormentor. His mother had been right. Hades had protected him. She had given him her strength. Joey tasted blood as his fangs crunched down on the babysitter's windpipe and tore it free.

NOTHING BETTER TO DO

Freddy was bored again. Slowly he slid slivers of wood into his anus shivering as the pain lanced up through his spine. He wasn't quite sure why he was doing it, but he had nothing better to do and it did take his mind off the soul numbing boredom of his life. He'd read that they'd found six-inch metal pins embedded in Albert Fish's rectum when they examined him after his capture. Freddy couldn't find any pins that long, but he did have some pretty long sewing needles. They didn't give him the same type of chills the splinters did though. The splinters set all his nerves on fire. Today, however, they just weren't doing the trick.

Freddy started to chew his nails, but there was no nail and little flesh left on his half-cannibalized phalanges. White bone stuck out from the top of each savaged finger. Freddy started chewing bits of dried and dead skin from his index finger wincing every time his teeth scraped bone. That's when he heard the dog; that over-sized, arthritic, asthmatic, poodle with the bleeding sores, and the whooping cough, that seemed to have been around forever. It was still alive! Freddy cursed aloud and slapped his hands over his ears to block out that horrible sound. Still, he could hear the dog's phlegm choked, tubercular cough coming from the next room, followed by a hoarse ragged bark that lead predictably back to a fit of coughing. Freddy wanted to yell at the dog to spit that damn phlegm out instead of continuing to swallow it. Just the thought of it made him ill.

That wet strangled cough was the worst sound Freddy could imagine. It made his stomach roll with nausea and grated on his nerves making him want to scream. Freddy began nervously chewing at his own bleeding nubs ignoring the sharp prickles of pain that each bite sent through his nervous system.

Freddy blamed all his obsessive compulsive behaviors on that mutant poodle. He had been torturing it for years and still it would not die. It still whispered in his ears every night; planting post-hypnotic suggestions like...shove splinters in your anus or chew off your fingertips. He hated the thing.

Once, Freddy had been looking through an old photo album and had been surprised to see that damned dog in almost every picture going back to his great-great grand mother. He could not help but to think about David Berkowitz, the Son of Sam, who had claimed that his neighbor's dog was a thousand-year-old demon who ordered him to kill. His grandparents had once lived next door to the Berkowitz family. They'd lived there right around the time the Son of Sam was rampaging across New York. Freddy was afraid that soon the dog would have enough control over him to make him a murderer too. He had to kill the thing. He'd taken a knife to it again yesterday yet the thing was still breathing and barking and coughing and eating and shitting all over the house!

Determined to end the poodle's dominion over his life, Freddy leapt from his bed, wincing as the needles in his asshole dug in deeper. He carefully bandaged his fingers; wrapping each torn appendage with pieces of toilet paper, not noticing that they were just as quickly bleeding through the makeshift Band-Aids. No more poison, no more guns, no more knives. Freddy would make sure the thing did not survive. He would burn it to death!

Freddy opened the door to his bedroom and walked out into the hallway, cursing aloud as he stepped directly into the wet, green and brown feces that covered every floor surface in the house.

"Fucking dog." He growled to himself.

He had to cover his face with a bath towel as the horrible, rancid pork smell of the half-dead, diseased dog, mixed with the smell of feces and roared up his nostrils, down his throat and into his stomach where it caused a tidal wave of bile and stomach acid. Freddy paused for a second as he fought to keep the wave from rising up his throat. Once his stomach was settled, he cautiously negotiated the obstacle course of dog shit and made his way to the kitchen where he knew the terrible creature would be.

"Hi Mom." Freddy said and dutifully bent over to plant a kiss on her withered cheek. The movement disturbed the legion of flies that had been planting eggs in her eye-sockets and feeding on the cocktail of bodily fluids evacuating her body. Her hair was moving, alive with maggots and still more flies. Her entire body was vibrating, seething with activity as dozens of carrion eating parasites were busily eating away at her flesh, taking her down to the bone.

Freddy yelled and kicked at the dog when he noticed that it had chewed off another of his mother's feet, taking most of the flesh from her one remaining shin as well. The dog yelped and retreated, dragging yards of bluish purple intestines with it from where Freddy had tried to disembowel it last year. As it barked, its brain flopped back and forth, threatening to spill from its exposed brainpan. Freddy had taken a few swings at it with a baseball bat sometime around Christmas. Its matted and filthy white fur was dotted with red from all the bullet holes Freddy had put into it over the years, and the hilt of a carving knife still protruded from its throat from Freddy's recent attempt to saw the thing's head off.

The hideously grotesque canine growled at him and backed away as he approached, limping and tripping over its intestines and leaking blood and bile all over the linoleum floor, adding to the mess already left by the piles of excrement from both the dog and Freddy's dead mother. Freddy could still remember the flood of urine and...and shit that had released from his Mom's bowels when he shot her as she tried to protect that damned poodle.

"He's been in the family forever! You can't kill it!"

"I know it's been here forever and don't you think there's something wrong about that? The damned thing won't die! Just look." He pointed the .357 Smith and Wesson revolver at the over-sized mutant poodle and his mother bent down to shield the thing. The bullet entered somewhere around mid-back and exited her solar plexus in an explosion of gore. She sat at the table, smoking one of those cheap generic cigarettes that smelled like charcoal and berating him for being a failure as a son as she bled to death. He listened to her vituperative tirade, each venomous word barely squeezing out between wheezing, whistling breaths from her ruptured lungs as they filled with blood and she slowly drowned. Her last words were something like:

"You pathetic waste of life! You should've been a stain on your daddy's sheets! And don't you dare hurt my dog!"

Immediately, Freddy had increased his efforts to kill the thing. The canine abomination was now feeding off the only thing in the house that had ever loved it.

"Ungrateful son-of-a-bitch! And she tried to protect you!" Freddy yelled.

The dog sat and began licking its ass in response.

There was a can of lighter fluid in the pantry and Freddy bent to retrieve it. The dog began to howl and bark before

59

succumbing to a horrific fit of coughing. It scrambled to the back door and scratched at the cheap aluminum, trying to claw right through it to freedom. It could sense that Freddy was up to something.

Freddy had the lighter fluid, the automatic log lighter and a devilish gleam in his eyes. He backed the dog into the corner and began dousing it with the accelerant.

"Don't do it, Freddy. You'll be sorry. I'll make you skin your own penis with a cheese grater tomorrow if you fuck with me!"

Freddy was used to the threats. He didn't care what the dog said. This would be its last day on earth. Freddy threw the match. He turned to get the fire extinguisher from under the sink as the dog began to howl and scream in indescribable agony. There was definitely something odd about the dog. Normal canines didn't scream or talk for that matter or live after they'd been stabbed, shot, bludgeoned, and disemboweled.

The dog was trying to bite at the flames. It's teeth were bared in a threatening snarl as it attacked the immediate source of its pain. The fire rapidly crawled up its back, shearing through the mangy tufts of hair as it began to consume the dog's living tissue. The little fat still clinging to the dog's emaciated body added fuel to the fire and furthered the progress of the flames. The poodle's flesh was starting to bubble and run like frying lard. Both of its eyes were sizzling in their sockets like sunny-side-up eggs. They exploded with an audible pop.

Freddy sprayed the dog with the fire extinguisher as soon as it stopped moving. He had to spray the walls as well as the fire had begun to spread up the drywall. Freddy cried out in joy as the blackened canine skeleton slumped to the floor. He negotiated his way through the festering piles of feces, back out of the kitchen, down the hall, and into his bedroom, pausing only to silence the wailing smoke alarms with a few whacks from his baseball bat. The house was now eerily quiet without the horrible coughing and hoarse barks. The only sound was the hum of flies on his mother's body, audible even through his closed bedroom door. Strangely enough, he found the sound soothing. It was like mom was humming him to sleep with some out of tune lullaby. Freddy laid down on his bed and felt years of pressure suddenly drop from his mind. The demon was dead. He fell into a deep contented sleep and dreamt of being a baby in his mother's arms, trying to remember what the milk from her mammoth breasts had tasted like.

When Freddy finally awakened hours later, it was to the same hoarse barking and wet, tubercular, phlegm-congested coughing that had greeted him every morning of his life. His left ear dripped with snot and saliva from where the wet nose of a thousand year old demon, the same one who had told David Berkowitz to take a .44 caliber pistol to couples on the streets of New York, had whispered in his ear as he slept. The ratty carpet had a trail of paw prints in black ash that led from his locked bedroom door to the edge of his bed. The damned thing had picked his lock again! Freddy cursed loudly as he reached for the cheese grater and began shredding the foreskin from his penis. He wasn't sure why he was doing it, but he had nothing better to do.

HOUSE CLEANING

Rosie patiently dusted the bookshelves; removing each book and wiping it down with an electrostatic rag and then replacing it precisely where it had been. She removed each knick-knack one at a time from the mantle and wiped it free of dust. Then she ran the feather duster over the smooth surface of the oak mantle before spraying it with furniture wax and buffing it to a high gloss.

"Filthy!" she hissed in disgust.

She wiped down the television and stereo system with the rag, spraying window cleaner on the screen and wiping it until her reflection shone through. She then threw the rag into the trashcan and grabbed another, repeating her frantic wiping on every piece of furniture, every knick-knack, and every trinket in the room. Everywhere she looked there was grime and scum, tops of the baseboards, beneath the stove and refrigerator, underneath the couch and between its cushions. She ran the vacuum slowly over the carpet until she was sure all the dust and dander was gone. Then she poured water and cleaning fluid into the steam cleaner and retraced her path over the carpet until it looked as if it had just come from the showroom floor. She poured three capfuls of ammonia into a bucket of water and lowered her mop down into it. Then she began furiously mopping the floors, walls, and ceiling.

When she was done the house shined like a show model.

Rosie appraised her work with admiration. Satisfied over her accomplishment she went upstairs and stripped off all of her clothing, dumping them into the washing machine along with a capful of laundry detergent. She looked her body over, sniffed her hands and armpits and wrinkled up her nose.

"Filthy!" she declared with undisguised revulsion.

She sprinted to the shower and began furiously scrubbing at her flesh, using various soaps and bath gels before grabbing the bottle of bleach and dumping it over her head, wincing in anticipation of the burn. Various cuts and abrasions sang out in agony as the bleach seared her flesh and she scrubbed herself raw. When she finally stepped from the shower, she smelled as fresh as new linen.

She dressed in fresh clothes and went out onto the porch to watch as the garbage man struggled to heft her two trashcans into the trash truck. She winced when he dropped one of the cans and piece after piece of her drunken adulterous husband tumbled out onto the sidewalk. Blood flooded from the upturned receptacle and stained the sidewalk crimson as first his head, eyes still wide in surprise, mouth open as if still trying to lie his way out of it, then his legs, arms and finally his bloated torso splattered onto the street behind the garbage truck. Blood rolled up onto the driveway in a wave as blood, organs, and intestines came boiling out of the tremendous gash bisecting the corpse's stomach and chest. Last, the gore-streaked weed whacker, the pruning shears, and the meat cleaver slid out of the garbage can on a slick trail of blood and viscera.

The two garbage men were shocked but managed to avoid throwing up and further soiling the blood-soaked street. They cautiously approached the second trashcan. The braver of the two stretched out his foot and kicked the can over, leaping back as the woman came sliding out leaving her skin and much of her flesh crumpled up at the bottom of the can. They both lost all pretense of bravery when the woman whose breasts, ass, and vagina had been removed, carved out so that the white of ribs and pelvic bone gleamed through where her sexual organs had been, turned eyes wide with terror towards them and began to scream. They hopped back into their truck and peeled out of the cul de sac, leaving the bloody mess behind.

"Filthy!" Rosie shrieked, her voice trembling with the force of judgement, tears beginning to well up in her eyes. She turned and went back into the house to collect her cleaning supplies.

FATTER

Tina looked in the mirror and felt her stomach roil with revulsion. She looked at her reflection and saw billowy rolls of adipose tissue dripping from each bloated appendage. She saw her own hideously distended torso enclustered with grotesque lumps of bulging fat and felt sickened. She didn't know how Hank could make love to this horrible corpulent cow; why anyone would want to. Her pudgy cheeks were so swollen that she could barely see her own squinty, piggish eyes. The image she saw staring back at her looked as if she'd been stung by a dozen bees, or like she had eaten bad seafood and was having an allergic reaction. Tina wanted to cry. She was getting fatter everyday.

Yesterday, she spent two-and-a-half hours on the treadmill. She had it in its highest gear and was turning red from both the exertion and the certainty that the people on the stationary bikes in back of her were laughing at the ripples she knew must be going through her massive ass. After the treadmill she'd gone to the weight-room for an hour, then to the sauna for forty-five minutes, and then ten-minutes in the bathroom regurgitating breakfast into the toilet bowl. Still, the image she saw in the mirror was no thinner.

Sometimes she thought about taking one of the knives from her kitchen and getting rid of the fat one cut at a time.

The only thing stopping her was the certainty that she would get too carried away and wind up taking too much off. It was better to let the professionals do it. She was already scheduled for her third lyposuction surgery. The fat just kept coming right back. The doctors said that this would be the last surgery. After that there would be nothing more they could do for her. If it didn't work this time... well, she wouldn't think about that right now.

Perhaps, the mirror was lying. She knew it could do that sometimes. Perhaps she was losing weight and didn't know it. She stared at the hideous lumps of cottage cheese flesh that hung from her engorged thighs and tried to see the slim beautiful person within. All she could think about, however, was how many layers of fat lay between her musculoskeletal system and her skin. She estimated that there must be a foot or so of superfluous tissue between where she began and where she ended. She wondered what it would feel like to be hugged without so much excess flesh between Hanks body and hers; what it would feel like to make love without what felt like a whole other person in bed between them. It was time to step on the scale.

Tina flexed her glutes, trying to keep them from jiggling as she crossed her bedroom floor and walked into her bathroom. The slight movement of her thighs as she walked, the even smaller jiggle that went through her buttocks, even the bounce of her breasts, appalled her. If the scale didn't tell her what she wanted to hear she *would* take that knife to herself. She crept across the cold vinyl floor and tapped the edge of the electronic scale with her big toe. She saw the screen light up and a row of zeroes line the liquid crystal display. Then she stepped both feet onto it and waited as it contemplated her body mass, preparing to give its verdict.

One hundred pounds. She gasped in astonishment and repeated the actions again. Stepping off the scale, tapping the clear button with her toe, stepping back onto the scale. One hundred pounds. She began to cry. Tears rolled down her smooth aquiline cheeks, down over the bones jutting from her chest, and between her withered breasts, over her protruding ribcage and concave stomach. They trailed over her sharp, painful looking pelvic bones and down her bony legs. She began to wail out loud.

"I'm still fat! Still fat! Still fat!" she screamed shaking her fist at the numbers blinking on the scale's display screen.

Once again, her weight had not changed at all. It was still in the triple digits. It was the same as it had been since she was eight years old. Back when the kids use to call her "Fat Girl" and "Lard Ass". She'd been dieting, and exercising, throwing up more than half of the few calories she ingested. She'd prayed, had surgery, and her weight was still the same. She was still that little fat girl the kids had made fun of.

Tina slowly pulled herself back together. She stepped calmly from the scale, wiped the tears from her eyes, balled her hands into tight fists, and took a deep breath; steeling her nerves. She knew what she had to do; the only way she would ever get that weight off. She walked into the kitchen and pulled the big Ginsu carving knife from the drawer. She looked at it, watched it shimmer and shine in the morning sun, then she shoved it back in the drawer and took out the slender filleting knife. She imagined what Hank would say when he saw her with all that disgusting fat finally off.

He was always telling her that she was beautiful, that she was just fine the way she was. He even tried to tell her that she was losing too much weight and needed to eat more. He pointed out other women on the street and in magazines and told her that she was skinnier than all of them. But Tina knew. She knew that no one was calling them "Lard Ass." She knew that Hank would love her more without the jiggling ass, and corpulent thighs, the hideous bulging layers of fat. She knew how to get rid of it all once and for all.

The blade cut deep and Tina had to bite down on a dishrag to keep her screams from being heard. She sawed deep; cutting through the flesh of her thighs and removing layers and layers of tissue. She'd been right of course. Once she started, she knew there was no way she could stop. She wanted it all gone. When she saw the gleaming white bone poke it's way through the layers of bloated flesh that had covered her thigh she smiled. Now all she had to do was get it off the rest of her body, then she would be skinny, then she would be happy, then no one would ever call her "Lard Ass" again, then Hank would never look at other women. She scraped the blade down her femur removing more and more flesh as she screamed into the dishrag and tears of joy ran down her face.

THE STRANGE LUSTS
OF HYPOCRITES

According to the priests and preachers and conservative moralists, everything about him was an abomination, a crime against God and nature. Mickey smiled and combed his long golden tresses out of his face with his painted and manicured talons. He applied another coat of lipstick to his full bee-stung lips, smoothed down the wrinkles on his velvet mini-skirt and adjusted his bra-strap. He was beautiful. No matter what the bible-thumpers said. Deep down, he knew that half the repressed cowards that condemned him secretly lusted for him. And why shouldn't they? He could do things for them that no woman could. He brushed his luxurious eyelashes with mascara and winked at himself in his hand-held mirror as a potential client rolled to a stop by the curb in front of him.

Mickey recognized the corpulent politician behind the wheel of the Mercedes. He'd seen the predatory hypocrite down there before. Hunting young street hustlers of both genders. The same gutter trash that he was lobbying hard to remove from the Boulevard. He'd watched him join televangelists on national television in denouncing the very behaviors he himself was addicted to. Often, the unfortunate victims of his lust would return to the strip with welts and bruises as evidence of the politician's peculiar passions. Mickey smiled and batted his long eyelashes at him.

"How much?"

"How much you got?"

Mickey waved his tight little ass at him and the man waved back with a hundred-dollar bill.

They entered a rundown one-bedroom flat with a warped and splintered wood floor and yellow, grease and cigarette-stained walls. There was a bed in the center of the room with a tattered, lice-ridden mattress stained with urine, semen, and blood. Mickey turned up his nose but turned to the politician and smiled.

"What does Daddy want?"

The fat politician's squinty little piggish eyes gleamed with hunger and delight as Mickey squeezed out of his mini-skirt and halter-top. Clients were sometimes taken aback when they discovered that he wasn't entirely female. But he knew that this pervert wouldn't mind. Just as he knew that the runes and symbols carved, branded, and tattooed across large portions of his flesh would only add to the thrill for this sadistic trick.

Mickey withstood the man's pawing and groping hands, endured his slimy tongue slathering his flesh in saliva. He allowed the man to spank him with a spiked paddle and flay his back with a cat o'nine tails before he revealed himself to him.

Mickey's skin opened up and he shrugged himself out of it. The politician began to scream as his eyes filled with the site of the monstrous creature uncoiling from Mickey's flesh. A serpentine body at once reptilian, insectile, and anthropoid, encrusted with scales, spikes, and horns, with a face dominated by a massive jaw like the mouth of some prehistoric reptile, scampered forward digging its polished and painted claws into the wood floor.

Mickey knew what the politician wanted. All Christians secretly lusted for the divine pleasures of hell. Pleasures for which Mickey's hell-spawned flesh had been expertly designed.

Mickey smiled at the puzzled look on the politician's face. His confusion was part of both his horror and his still undiminished lust. He could see the politician's mind desperately trying to make sense of Mickey's arcane anatomy; part human, part dragon, part praying mantis, even as he began blubbering and crying like a child as Mickey cornered him on the bed and reached for his still oddly erect penis.

Mickey's smooth scaly hands crawled over the politician's throbbing cock and his tremendous mandibles parted wide to consume the tender organ. Mickey smiled revealing rows of fangs as his true sexual organs writhed like a nest of tentacles between his thighs and reached out for the politician, coiling around his body and slowly constricting him even as they began to enter him, finding orifices even this jaded libertine would have never conceived of. The politician's screams became piercing shrieks as his erection went between those lethal jaws and down Mickey's throat

Mickey fucked him violently, mercilessly, ripping into his puckered anus, ejaculating his scalding black seed down his throat filling up his mouth until it spilled across his cheeks and dribbled down his chin. Mickey was not surprised when the politician's screams turned to sultry moans and he began to convulse in the throes of a violent orgasm, no longer caring about his soul which Mickey was eagerly sucking out through his swollen cock, too lost in the rapturous agony of myriad voluptuous sins.

"Oh my God you are incredible! I love you! More! Give me more!"

Fucking hypocrites. They were all the same.

71

AFTER THE CURE

It looked like a staple gun or something you used to shoot penny nails into two-by-fours. I felt a shivering fear rake it's icy nails up my spine as the nurse swabbed my arm with alcohol and brought the lethal looking contraption down to the thick pulsing vein on the inside of my elbow. There was a bluish green vial on top of the gun and I watched as the 40-year-old, surgically rejuvenated nurse, pulled the trigger and the algae colored vaccine shot down into my veins. The cure. A shit load of adrenaline coursed through my veins. I felt like superman. The motherfucking cure! I was invincible now! I would live forever!

I wanted to fuck the entire world, including the silicone enhanced, peroxide blonde, big-bootied nurse, who had the hardened look of a street prostitute several birthdays past her prime. She had that deep line on either side of her mouth that I always associated with giving too many blowjobs. Right now, after a decade and a half of fear and dick shriveling precautions, latex, spermicides, awkward interviews/interrogations about past lovers and sex practices, anyone and everyone was fuckable. There was about to be a worldwide sexual revolution that would make the birth control pill and the '60s free-love movement look puritanical, and I was gonna be a part of it!

"You might experience a few side effects for the first few days but it should be nothing worse than a bad cold and generally no more than a runny nose. If you experience anything more serious than that please call us right away."

The cure came in the form of a genetically altered cold virus, a mutant virus designed to attack and destroy other viruses. It attacks the HIV virus even while it's hidden inside a white blood cell, but without damaging the cell itself or any other system in the body. This new cannibal virus also has the wonderful side affect of attacking any virus that enters the body making you nearly immune to any viral infection which includes nearly every known STD and even the non-mutated cold virus. The cure for AIDS and the common cold all in one blow.

For some reason the idea of fucking this old chick in the ass had gotten into my head and I just couldn't seem to shake it. She turned and looked me full in the face and licked her lips. I was tempted to bend her over the examination table.

"You want to fuck me don't you?" She was staring at my growing erection with a look that could only have been described as hunger.

"Uh...um."

"It's okay. I've noticed the vaccine seems to have that effect on people. Go lock the door."

The moment was so surreal. I stumbled along like I was in a dream as I walked over and locked the door. When I turned back, she had her huge double D breasts already out of her bra and her skirt pulled up to her waist. Her panty hose were down around her ankles. She reached out and grabbed my belt with one hand and my zipper with the other. In seconds she had my pants down to my knees and my dick halfway down her throat.

She was slurping and sucking like a newborn on its mother's tit. She pulled my cock out of her mouth and began licking it up and down while she stroked it with her hand, sucking and licking my balls and playing with her pussy. She sucked my dick down her throat again. I watched as each inch disappeared. I could still feel her tongue twirling around the shaft. A truly talented woman. I felt like I was about to explode right down her throat. I reached down and brought her to her feet. Then I turned her around and bent her over the examining room table. I reached down into my pocket and fiddled for my condoms. She turned and smacked them out of my hands.

"Now what the fuck do you need those for? You've got the cure remember? And I'm on the pill. I want to feel you inside me."

Remembering that I no longer needed condoms added iron to my erection. I bent her over the table and thrust my cock up into her tight pussy. I reached around and grabbed hold of her tremendous breasts as I slammed my engorged cock in and out of her dripping wet pussy. She had amazing muscle control. Her kegel muscles gripped my shaft, milking it. My nuts slapped against her large round ass as I tried to drive up into her guts. She had one of those little dressing gowns shoved in her mouth to keep from screaming out loud, but I was certain her moans could be heard beyond the door.

Her kegels tightened as she came, thrashing and shaking. Her moans were so loud now that I was sure everyone in the clinic must have heard us. I pulled my dick, sopping wet with her juices, out of her and slid it into her ass. She let out a sound like an animal growling as I thrust deep in her puckered anus. She fingered her clit while I pounded into her and in seconds she was coming again. Her sphincter tightened around my dick and the sensation was almost overwhelming. Blood rushed to my head and for a moment I was afraid I was going to faint.

"Oh my God, baby. I don't know if I can take your big

old dick in my ass. Here, give me that."

She slid my erection out of her ass just as I was starting to speed up my rhythm, slamming my cock into her ass up to my nuts. She turned around and knelt down gripping my dick between her breasts and began sliding it up and down her cleavage as she licked the head of my cock. I grabbed the top of her head and fucked her enormous tits. I felt a tingling in my balls that spread up though my dick as the orgasm ripped through me like gunfire. Again and again gouts of warm, white semen splashed onto her breasts and all over her face as she continued to lick the head of my dick. She emptied me, lapping and gobbling up my cum as I came for what seemed like an eternity. I would have done Peter North proud. Her face looked like the bottom of a milk pail, like a painter's shoes.

She raised each of her tremendous breasts to her lips and licked my semen from her nipples like a kitten lapping milk from a saucer. Her tongue flickered up and down my shaft then swirled around the head of my cock, licking it clean. She smiled up at me with her face still glistening with semen.

"You know how long it's been since I drank cum? This vaccine is gonna open up a whole new world for me!"

I slid my pants back up and buckled them.

"I'm happy for you."

I suddenly felt uncomfortable and claustrophobic in the little examining room. It was not an unfamiliar sensation. I always feel like that after an orgasm. I'm not the type to stay and chat or cuddle. When I'm done, I'm done.

I put my leather motorcycle jacket on, turned and left. She was still pulling up her panty hose when the next patient was led in. I wondered if he was in line for the same treatment. Now that venereal disease was a thing of the past, who could blame her? Amazingly, my dick had already gotten hard again...very hard. Without underwear, it bulged

shamelessly in my over-sized Hugo Boss jeans. I strolled out
of the examination room into the lobby, with my eyes glazed
with lust. I scanned the line of people who filled the Haight
Ashbury Free Clinic, looking for someone with whom to
share my addiction. The hunger was already back upon me.

My eyes fell upon a diminutive Winona Rider look-a-like
with breasts so large they seemed to be nearly half her body
weight. She was wearing a black motorcycle jacket similar
to mine, overtop a thin white tank top through which her
large round breasts were clearly visible. The tiny hard nipples
seemed to be pointing right at me. Her eyes clouded over with
that smoky hypnotic lust that identified her as a fellow sex
addict, even as her clothing identified her as a lesbian.

She wore tight, black Levis with a thick leather belt. A
small chain led from her belt loop to the leather wallet in
her pocket. She had about six little silver hoop earrings in
her right ear and four in the left. On her leather jacket was
a small pink triangle. I normally tried to steer clear of my
kindred addicts as they represented a high-risk group, but as
lesbians were at the lowest risk for AIDS, I had often made
exceptions where they were concerned. I looked at the small
cotton swab taped to the inside of my arm and thought to
myself that it was all a moot point now.

I returned her gaze with an equally lascivious look
complete with a head to toe appraisal. We both smiled.
I turned and walked down the steps onto Haight Street. I
looked at the line that trailed all the way down the steps of
the free clinic, out the door, and down the street, all the way
to the Panhandle. I saw a guy that I knew from the clubs
standing in line with his girlfriend. I wasn't sure whether
that was sweet or just tacky.

"Yo, what's up Ali?" I said.

"'Sup, Shark? You got yours already?"

"Yeah, bro. I ain't even been to sleep yet. I been in line

since I got off work at two in the morning and there were still like two hundred people ahead of me."

"Yeah, you oughta been." Ali whipped his neat, perfectly, groomed dreadlocks back out of his face and flashed his feline, almond eyes at the scrawny little white girl with the mousy brown hair that clung to his arm like it was a life line. She was so pale she could have gotten a sunburn indoors at night.

"What do you mean by that?"

"I'm sayin' you done fucked half the bitches in this town. It's a wonder you ain't dead already. You's one lucky muthafucka."

"It's not luck, dude." I held up a six pack of Trojan Magnums. "I live in Latex."

I knew there were rumors going around about my sexual exploits. The chains with the leather restraints that hung from the ceiling in the living room of my apartment didn't help matters. I put them up there when I was dating this stripper who was heavy into S&M and B&D. I'm not really as sexually extravagant as people think. My tastes are pretty simple. I like to fuck. Where, how, and who doesn't really matter that much. I'm open-minded. If a girl wants me to tie her up and whip her that's cool as long as the night ends with my nuts slapping against her ass and my cum dripping off her chin. My preference is sex as opposed to no sex.

"I hear that shit. What's up for tonight?" Ali asked. His girlfriend was still attached to his side like some kind of 112 pound parasite. She stared out at me with huge wide eyes and her expression seemed to change along with Ali's. She never said a word. The chick was weird.

"I got a cult meeting tonight."

"A cult meeting?"

"Yeah, you know...Sex Addicts Anonymous. My daily reprogramming session."

"It don't look like that shit is working. I heard you got thrown out of the Sound Factory last night for fucking one of the cocktail waitresses behind the speakers."

"She told me no one goes back there. Dude, there was like three other couples back there. Security swooped down on us before I could even get my nut off."

Ali rolled his eyes and shook his head.

"Yeah, that's a real tragedy." He replied sarcastically, "Hey, yo, the line's moving. I'll peep you later."

"Cool."

The young raven-haired lesbian emerged from the clinic. Her breasts were bobbling around under her T-shirt like a bag of basketballs, the nipples poked through like tiny pink darts. I turned to look her full in the face as she walked up towards me, smiling up at me from chest level.

"What's your name, beautiful?" I asked.

"Simon."

"Simone?"

"No, Simon." She said forcefully.

"Alright. That's cool. My name is Shark."

"Shark?"

"Yeah,"

"Is that your real name? I mean is that what your mother named you?"

I looked at her like she was an idiot.

"Stupid question, huh? Well, it doesn't matter anyway."

I smiled, trying hard not to let too much of my lust show through in the expression. Still, I jumped right to the point. I knew what she was and she knew what I was. There was no need for formalities between sex addicts.

"You have anywhere you need to be?"

She shrugged,

"Not for about two hours."

Our eyes burned into each other and I noticed her pelvis

was making small circles, humping the air, even as I noticed that mine was doing the same. I could almost smell the taste of her arousal. My erection was clearly visible, forming a tent beneath my baggy Hugo Boss jeans. She reached out and casually traced her finger down the length of my manhood without breaking eye contact.

"Let's go to my place." I said

"We'll take my car," She replied. We could both barely suppress the urge to run to her little white '79 Volvo, parked on the other side of Haight street.

My senses were on fire with want. The ride from the free clinic to my apartment was only four blocks but I'd already unbuttoned her pants and slid my hands down between her legs into her silky wetness. I had two fingers sliding in and out of her pussy while my thumb flicked back and forth over her clit. She reached over and unzipped my pants, pulling my engorged member out of my pants, stroking it with her right hand while still driving with her left. I continued to finger her wet little pussy.

We pulled up into the driveway of my apartment. I couldn't wait until we got inside. I wanted her now. I pulled my pants completely off as we sat in the car. She looked at me quizzically, then smiled, leaned over, and swallowed the whole length of my erection, taking all nine inches down her throat. I was amazed. I could feel her tonsils. Her head bobbed up and down slowly at first then faster. Her lips and tongue slid along the smooth skin of my bloated organ accompanied by her hand, which had the shaft of my cocked gripped firmly. I played with her nipples and watched her beautiful face as she pleasured me. A tingling sensation went from my balls to the base of my cock. I lifted her head from my groin, dislodging my cock from her mouth with an audible "Slurp!". It was too soon to cum. I reached my hands under her arms and lifted her onto my turgid flesh.

"Wait!"

"What?"

"Do you have a condom?"

She began to laugh and my own booming laughter joined in. With the exception of pregnancy, for which there had long been an antidote, we would never again need a condom for any reason. It was such a liberating realization that it seemed to arouse us both even greater. I lowered her onto me, feeling the wetness of her, the tightness of her, the delicious sensations of flesh cocooned within flesh that no condom or lubricant could come close to simulating. She bounced up and down on my dick, pounding it deep inside her as we fucked furiously in her little Volvo. I clutched her tiny hips and pulled her even deeper. She let out a little squeal as I pushed up into her guts. She pulled off her T-shirt, revealing the most magnificent set of titties I'd ever seen. I greedily sucked and licked at her hard little nipples as her breasts bounced up and down to our rhythm, slapping me in my face. The little Volvo rocked and swayed.

Way past giving a fuck, I opened the car door and stepped out, butt naked, with her legs wrapped around my waist, as I continued to thrust deep inside her. Our lips were sealed together as our tongues dueled. I was only peripherally aware of the stares and gasps of amazement. We were drawing a crowd. Cars stopped. Neighbors peeked from open windows. Pedestrians paused on the street. There were cheers, clapping, cat-calls, and whistles. There were a few threats and admonishments, fewer than I would have expected, and those were quickly shouted down by the crowd. I smiled at them and continued fucking Simon, spurred on by the crowd. One of the spectators, a skinny hippy in a Grateful Dead t-shirt, was brazenly masturbating as he watched us. A man in a business suit took the cue and began stroking himself through his pants before finally pulling his cock out and openly flagellating himself. A middle-aged woman with breasts even larger than Simon's, removed her shirt and hiked up her skirt. She slid her hand down into her panties and began fingering herself. It was getting weird. A young couple that I recognized from the line outside the Free Clinic, laid down on the sidewalk and began fucking. There was definitely something in that vaccine, something that destroyed normal inhibitions. I had a moment to wonder if society would breakdown if all the taboos and societal mores that kept us civilized were to suddenly disintegrate rather than the gradual erosion we had grown accustomed to, then my thoughts turned back to Simon who was still straddling my erection.

My apartment was in the basement of a house on the corner of Haight and Masonic Street that was three stories high with each floor separated into individual flats. Mine had its own private entrance through the back that led directly into my bedroom. With Simon still wrapped around my dick, I pulled my house key from the flowerpot where I always left it. We stepped into my flat and directly into the bedroom. There was an immediate sigh of disappointment and a spattering of boos from the crowd outside. I turned my head and took one last look at them before I shut the door, just in time to see the masturbating hippie shoot an arc of semen onto a woman's pink open-toed heels. The woman didn't seem to mind at all. She smiled at him with a peculiar hunger in her eyes. The woman who'd taken off her shirt was now jacking off the guys standing on either side of her as they sucked and fondled her breasts. Shit was definitely getting weirder. I almost wanted to stay and watch. Hesitantly, I closed the door.

I lifted Simon from me, temporarily breaking our bond as I laid her on the bed. She raised her legs into the air and spread them wide, beckoning me to her. She cupped my face in her hands and guided my mouth down to the silky, sweet, wetness between her thighs. I lapped up her juices, sucking her clit and plunging my tongue deep into her as she gasped and sighed, legs quivering. Her moans fueled my hunger. I flicked my tongue across her clit like a buzzsaw, driving her crazy. Her fingers gripped my head tightly as she ground her sex into my face, smothering me. I couldn't breathe, but I didn't care. I wanted to die inside of her, to drown in her juices.

When she came, it was like a tidal wave splashing down over my tongue. Her body rocked and bucked. Her fingernails clawed at the sheets and the veins in her neck stood out. A small scream strained its way out between her clenched teeth. Her orgasm was so powerful I nearly came myself. After the last wave of orgasm rippled through her body she guided me up from between her legs and up over her head until my chest was against her lips. She licked and sucked my nipples sending salacious chills down to the root of my manhood. Just when I was quivering on the edge of madness, she reached down and grabbed my dick in her two hands, stroking while still sucking at my chest. I was about to explode. Once again, she guided me up over her head until I was on all fours with my dick pressed against her lips, seconds from orgasm. She rolled her tongue around the tip of my swollen organ, bathing it in her saliva. With one hand, she reached around to cup my tight muscular ass and to pull me closer so that my dick slid down her throat, all nine inches disappearing 'til her lips were buried in my pubic hair. I could feel her throat constricting around the head of my cock. I began to thrust in and out of her mouth, fucking her face, my balls slapping against her chin. I came, a volcanic eruption that racked my body with spasms and emptied me. My semen filled her mouth and spilled out over her cheeks, dripping from her lips down her chin and neck.

She pulled my dick out of her mouth and squeezed the last of my cum onto her outstretched tongue. She licked her lips then used her index finger to scoop my semen from her face and neck and into her mouth, where she licked her fingers clean as well. My erection barely diminished. She sucked and licked it until it jumped back to huge throbbing life.

I turned her over on all fours and entered her wet pussy in the position customary to mammals, pounding into her with renewed vigor. I could feel her muscles contract around my cock, sucking me deeper into her. She rocked backwards onto my dick, her ass slapping against my thighs and sending ripples through each cheek. I spanked her sweet little ass. She gasped and grunted and pushed her ass back even further.

When she came she screamed again and this time she cried. Her body convulsed and the spasms brought me to my own climax. It was the first time in years I'd actually cum inside a woman. It was heaven! We collapsed to the bed and held each other like two long lost lovers reunited. Then we laughed long and uncontrollably. We were alive. We had the cure.

Outside, the sounds of passion echoed like they were being broadcast from a stereo system with the amplifier turned up to ten. It sounded like the entire city was fucking.

"What's going on?" Simon asked.

"Let's go check."

We crept over to a bedroom window and peered out at the street. It was chaos. At first I thought I was watching a riot. There were bodies strewn across the sidewalk, on the hood of cars, inside cars with doors open, in the middle of the street, bodies in various stages of undress entwined, kneeling, laying, squatting, sitting, on all fours, on their bellies, in every position imaginable. It took my mind a moment to adjust before it became clear. They were fucking. Everywhere. Everyone furiously fucking. An orgy that stretched as far as the eye could see in all directions. It was a sex addict's paradise.

"Come on!"

I took Simon's hand and we ran out into the street, still naked into the sweating, moaning, undulating tide of humanity. Immediately, I felt a dozen hands groping for me, stroking and caressing. I felt their wet mouths, their lips, tongues, breasts, and penises all over me and I fell down among them, taken away by the greatest aphrodisiac the world has ever known. Hope. Freedom. After decades of fear, decades of worry and caution, we were finally liberated. We had the cure.

We fucked long into the night, pleasure became pain as flesh began to chafe and then to tear and bleed. More people came to join us and soon it became clear that we could not stop. Whatever they injected us with was more than the cure to AIDS, more than a cure for STDS, it had stimulated something in our brains, in the most primal region of the amagdala where our sexual desire and our survival instincts were housed and caused a riot there. The desire to eat, to sleep, to drink had all been suppressed in favor of one lone instinct. Procreation. Again and again we expelled our bodily fluids without replacing them, even pausing to drink was no longer an option.

The day ended and became night and then day again and we continued fucking. In agony, our bodies crashed together, bleeding, screaming, but still vigorously, furiously fucking.

"I love you, Simon."

"I love you too, Shark."

"Mark. My real name is Mark."

"I love you too, Mark."

I didn't mean it and neither did she. It just seemed like the right thing to say. I'd fucked more than a dozen women more than a hundred times in the last twenty-four hours yet I kept coming back to her, drawn to her. I was certain that I would die with her and that it wouldn't be long. My last ejaculation had been almost entirely blood. Her vagina and anus was now just a ragged bleeding maw sopping and dripping with the semen of countless men, still I thrust into it in a maniacal fervor. My lungs burned, my muscles ached, and my penis had sloughed off most of its skin. I looked into Simon's eyes and laughed.

Twenty-four hours ago, we both thought we would live forever, that the cure would make us invincible. Now, we were going to fuck each other to death. She laughed too then screamed as another orgasm ripped through her starving dehydrated body and she continued to fuck me.

MAKE LOVE TO ME

Make love to me
I want to scream in the lascivious agonies
of your love

Burn me alive
in the voluptuous heat
of your eyes

Shatter my skull
With the ballistic speed
of your tongue

Make Love to Me

I want to perish
impaled on your tongue

I want to drown
in your desires

I want to sacrifice myself
on the altar
of your sex

I want to die
in the gleam
of your eyes

ABOUT THE AUTHOR

WRATH JAMES WHITE is a former World Class Heavyweight Kickboxer, a professional Kickboxing and Mixed Martial Arts trainer, distance runner, performance artist, and former street brawler, who is now known for creating some of the most disturbing works of fiction in print .

Wrath's two most recent novels are THE RESURRECTIONIST and YACCUB'S CURSE. He is also the author of SUCCULENT PREY, EVERYONE DIES FAMOUS IN A SMALL TOWN, THE BOOK OF A THOUSAND SINS, HIS PAIN and POPULATION ZERO. He is the coauthor of TERATOLOGIST cowritten with the king of extreme horror, Edward Lee, ORGY OF SOULS cowritten with Maurice Broaddus, HERO cowritten with J.F. Gonzalez, and POISONING EROS cowritten with Monica J. O'Rourke.

Wrath lives and works in Austin, Texas with his two daughters, Isis and Nala, his son Sultan and his wife Christie.

deadite
press

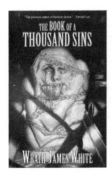

"The Book of a Thousand Sins" Wrath James White - Welcome to a world of Zombie nymphomaniacs, psychopathic deities, voodoo surgery, and murderous priests. Where mutilation sex clubs are in vogue and torture machines are sex toys. No one makes it out alive – not even God himself.

"If Wrath James White doesn't make you cringe, you must be riding in the wrong end of a hearse."
-Jack Ketchum

"Population Zero" Wrath James White - An intense sadistic tale of how one man will save the world through sterilization. *Population Zero* is the story of an environmental activist named Todd Hammerstein who is on a mission to save the planet. In just 50 years the population of the planet is expected to double. But not if Todd can help it. From Wrath James White, the celebrated master of sex and splatter, comes a tale of environmentalism, drugs, and genital mutilation.

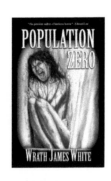

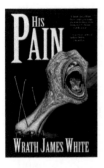

"His Pain" Wrath James White - Life is pain . . . . . . or at least it is for Jason. Born with a rare central nervous disorder, every sensation is pain. Every sound, scent, texture, flavor, even every breath, brings nothing but mind-numbing pain. Until the arrival of Yogi Arjunda of the Temple of Physical Enlightenment. He claims to be able to help Jason, to be able to give him a life of more than agony. But the treatment leaves Jason changed and he wants to share what he learned. He wants to share his pain . . . A novella of pain, pleasure, and transcendental splatter.

"The Vegan Revolution . . . with Zombies" David Agranoff - Thanks to a new miracle drug the cute little pig no longer feels a thing as she is led to the slaughter. The only problem? Once the drug enters the food supply anyone who eats it is infected. From fast food burgers to free-range organic eggs, eating animal products turns people into shambling brain-dead zombies – not even vegetarians are safe!

"A perfect blend of horror, humor and animal activism."
- Gina Ranalli

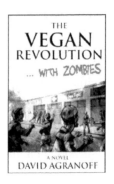

"Whargoul" Dave Brockie - It is a beast born in bullets and shrapnel, feeding off of pain, misery, and hard drugs. Cursed to wander the Earth without the hope of death, it is reborn again and again to spread the gospel of hate, abuse, and genocide. But what if it's not the only monster out there? What if there's something worse? From Dave Brockie, the twisted genius behind GWAR, comes a novel about the darkest days of the twentieth century.

"Super Fetus" Adam Pepper - Try to abort this fetus and he'll kick your ass!

"The story of a self-aware fetus whose morally bankrupt mother is desperately trying to abort him. This darkly humorous novella will surely appall and upset a sizable percentage of people who read it . . . In-your-face, allegorical social commentary."

 - BarnesandNoble.com

"Slaughterhouse High" Robert Devereaux - It's prom night in the Demented States of America. A place where schools are built with secret passageways, rebellious teens get zippers installed in their mouths and genitals, and once a year one couple is slaughtered and the bits of their bodies are kept as souvenirs. But something's gone terribly wrong when the secret killer starts claiming a far higher body count than usual . . .
"A major talent!" - Poppy Z. Brite

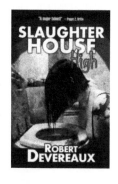

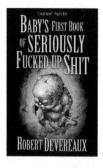

"Baby's First Book of Seriously Fucked-Up Shit" Robert Devereaux - From an orgy between God, Satan, Adam and Eve to beauty pageants for fetuses. From a giant human-absorbing tongue to a place where God is in the eyes of the psychopathic. This is a party at the furthest limits of human decency and cruelty. Robert Devereaux is your host but watch out, he's spiked the punch with drugs, sex, and dismemberment. Deadite Press is proud to present nine stories of the strange, the gross, and the just plain fucked up.

THE VERY BEST IN CULT HORROR

deadite press

"Urban Gothic" Brian Keene - When their car broke down in a dangerous inner-city neighborhood, Kerri and her friends thought they would find shelter inside an old, dark row home. They thought they would be safe there until help arrived. They were wrong. The residents who live down in the cellar and the tunnels beneath the city are far more dangerous than the streets outside, and they have a very special way of dealing with trespassers. Trapped in a world of darkness, populated by obscene abominations, they will have to fight back if they ever want to see the sun again.

"Jack's Magic Beans" Brian Keene - It happens in a split-second. One moment, customers are happily shopping in the Save-A-Lot grocery store. The next instant, they are transformed into bloodthirsty psychotics, interested only in slaughtering one another and committing unimaginably atrocious and frenzied acts of violent depravity. Deadite Press is proud to bring one of Brian Keene's bleakest and most violent novellas back into print once more. This edition also includes four bonus short stories.

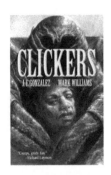

"Clickers" J. F. Gonzalez and Mark Williams- They are the Clickers, giant venomous blood-thirsty crabs from the depths of the sea. The only warning to their rampage of dismemberment and death is the terrible clicking of their claws. But these monsters aren't merely here to ravage and pillage. They are being driven onto land by fear. Something is hunting the Clickers. Something ancient and without mercy. *Clickers* is J. F. Gonzalez and Mark Williams' gore-soaked cult classic tribute to the giant monster B-movies of yesteryear.

"Clickers II" J. F. Gonzalez and Brian Keene- Thousands of Clickers swarm across the entire nation and march inland, slaughtering anyone and anything they come across. But this time the Clickers aren't blindly rushing onto land - they are being led by an intelligence older than civilization itself. A force that wants to take dry land away from the mammals. Those left alive soon realize that they must do everything and anything they can to protect humanity – no matter the cost. *This isn't war, this is extermination.*

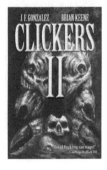

"A Gathering of Crows" Brian Keene - Five mysterious figures are about to pay a visit to Brinkley Springs. They have existed for centuries, emerging from the shadows only to destroy. To kill. To feed. They bring terror and carnage, and leave blood and death in their wake. The only person that can prevent their rampage is ex-Amish magus Levi Stoltzfus. As the night wears on, Brinkley Springs will be quiet no longer. Screams will break the silence. But when the sun rises again, will there be anyone left alive to hear?

"Take the Long Way Home" Brian Keene - All across the world, people suddenly vanish in the blink of an eye. Gone. Steve, Charlie and Frank were just trying to get home when it happened. Trapped in the ultimate traffic jam, they watch as civilization collapses, claiming the souls of those around them. God has called his faithful home, but the invitations for Steve, Charlie and Frank got lost. Now they must set off on foot through a nightmarish post-apocalyptic landscape in search of answers. In search of God. In search of their loved ones. And in search of home.

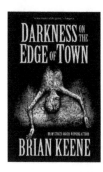

"Darkness on the Edge of Town" Brian Keene - One morning the residents of Walden, Virginia, woke up to find the rest of the world gone. Surrounding their town was a wall of inky darkness, plummeting Walden into permanent night. Nothing can get in - not light, not people, not even electricity, radio, TV, internet, food, or water. And nothing can get out. No one who dared to penetrate the mysterious barrier has ever been seen again. But for some, the darkness is not the worst of their fears.

"Tequila's Sunrise" Brian Keene - Discover the secret origins of the "drink of the gods" in this dark fantasy fable by best-selling author Brian Keene. Chalco, a young Aztec boy, feels helpless as conquering Spanish forces near his village. But when a messenger of the gods hands him a key to unlock the doors of human perception and visit unseen worlds, Chalco journeys into the mystical Labyrinth, searching for a way to defeat the invaders. He will face gods, devils, and things that are neither. But he will also learn that some doorways should never be opened and not all entrances have exits...

AVAILABLE FROM AMAZON.COM

deadite press

"Brain Cheese Buffet" Edward Lee - collecting nine of Lee's most sought after tales of violence and body fluids. Featuring the Stoker nominated "Mr. Torso," the legendary gross-out piece "The Dritiphilist," the notorious "The McCrath Model SS40-C, Series S," and six more stories to test your gag reflex.

"Edward Lee's writing is fast and mean as a chain saw revved to full-tilt boogie."
      - Jack Ketchum

"Bullet Through Your Face" Edward Lee - No writer is more extreme, perverted, or gross than Edward Lee. His world is one of psychopathic redneck rapists, sex addicted demons, and semen stealing aliens. Brace yourself, the king of splatterspunk is guaranteed to shock, offend, and make you laugh until you vomit.

"Lee pulls no punches."
      - Fangoria

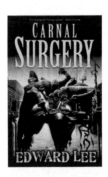

"Carnal Surgery" Edward Lee - Autopsy fetishes, crippled sex slaves, a serial killer who keeps the hands of his victims, government conspiracies, dead cops and doomed pornographers. From operating room morality plays to a town that serves up piss and cum mixed drinks, this is the strange and disturbing world of Edward Lee. From one of the most notorious, controversial, and extreme voices in horror fiction comes a new collection of depravity and terror. Carnal Surgery collects eleven of Lee's most sought after tales of sex and dismemberment.

"Trolley No. 1852" Edward Lee - In 1934, horror writer H.P. Lovecraft is invited to write a story for a subversive underground magazine, all on the condition that a pseudonym will be used. The pay is lofty, and God knows, Lovecraft needs the money. There's just one catch. It has to be a pornographic story . . . The 1852 Club is a bordello unlike any other. Its women are the most beautiful and they will do anything. But there is something else going on at this sex club. In the back rooms monsters are performing vile acts on each other and doors to other dimensions are opening . . .

"The Haunter of the Threshold" Edward Lee - There is something very wrong with this backwater town. Suicide notes, magic gems, and haunted cabins await her. Plus the woods are filled with monsters, both human and otherworldly. And then there are the horrible tentacles . . . Soon Hazel is thrown into a battle for her life that will test her sanity and sex drive. The sequel to H.P. Lovecraft's The Haunter of the Dark is Edward Lee's most pornographic novel to date!

"The Innswich Horror" Edward Lee - In July, 1939, antiquarian and H.P. Lovecraft aficionado, Foster Morley, takes a scenic bus tour through northern Massachusetts and finds Innswich Point. There far too many similarities between this fishing village and the fictional town of Lovecraft's masterpiece, The Shadow Over Innsmouth. Join splatter king Edward Lee for a private tour of Innswich Point - a town founded on perversion, torture, and abominations from the sea.

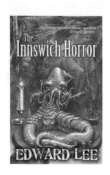

"Mangled Meat" Edward Lee - No writer is more hardcore, offensive, or notorious than Edward Lee. His world is one of torture, bizarre fetishes, and alien autopsies. Prepare yourself, as these three novellas from the king of splatterspunk are guaranteed to make you gasp, gag, and laugh your ass off. Featuring "The Decortication Technician," "The Cyesolagniac," and "Room 415."

"Apeshit" Carlton Mellick III - Friday the 13th meets Visitor Q. Six hipster teens go to a cabin in the woods inhabited by a deformed killer. An incredibly fucked-up parody of B-horror movies with a bizarro slant
"The new gold standard in unstoppable fetus-fucking kill-freakomania . . . Genuine all-meat hardcore horror meets unadulterated Bizarro brainwarp strangeness. The results are beyond jaw-dropping, and fill me with pure, unforgivable joy." - John Skipp

THE VERY BEST IN CULT HORROR

deadite press

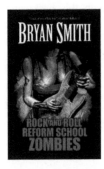

"Rock and Roll Reform School Zombies" Bryan Smith - Sex, Death, and Heavy Metal! The Southern Illinois Music Reeducation Center specializes in "de-metaling" – a treatment to cure teens of their metal loving, devil worshiping ways. A program that subjects its prisoners to sexual abuse, torture, and brain-washing. But tonight things get much worse. Tonight the flesh-eating zombies come . . . *Rock and Roll Reform School Zombies* is Bryan Smith's tribute to "Return of the Living Dead" and "The Decline of Western Civilization Part 2: the Metal Years."

"Highways to Hell" Bryan Smith - The road to hell is paved with angels and demons. Brain worms and dead prostitutes. Serial killers and frustrated writers. Zombies and Rock 'n Roll. And once you start down this path, there is no going back. Collecting thirteen tales of shock and terror from Bryan Smith, Highways to Hell is a non-stop road-trip of cruelty, pain, and death. Grab a seat, Smith has such sights to show you.

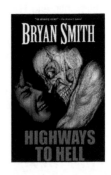

"The Killing Kind" Bryan Smith - Roxie is the goth girl of your dreams. There's just one problem-she's batshit crazy and has a fetish for murder. After a petty insult at a gas station, she goes on a murder spree, hunting down those that pissed her off. But she's not the only monster on the road. There are others out there killing and raping. And everyone's headed to the same beach house. A desolate vacation getaway with no neighbors and no one to hear the screams.

"Zombies and Shit" Carlton Mellick III - *Battle Royale* meets *Return of the Living Dead* in this post-apocalyptic action adventure. Twenty people wake to find themselves in a boarded-up building in the middle of the zombie wasteland. They soon realize they have been chosen as contestants on a popular reality show called Zombie Survival. Each contestant is given a backpack of supplies and a unique weapon. Their goal: be the first to make it through the zombie-plagued city to the pick-up zone alive. A campy, trashy, punk rock gore fest.

"Piecemeal June" Jordan Krall - Kevin lives in a small apartment above a porn shop with his tarot-reading cat, Mithra.She brings him things from outside and one day-brings him an rubber-latex ankle... Later an eyeball, then a foot. After more latex body parts are brought upstairs, Kevin glues them together to form a piecemeal sex doll. But once the last piece is glued into place, the sex doll comes to life. She says her name is June. She comes from another world and is on the run from an evil pornographer and three crab-human hybrid assassins.

"Fistful of Feet" Jordan Krall - A bizarro tribute to Spaghetti westerns, H.P. Lovecraft, and foot fetish enthusiasts. Screwhorse, Nevada is legendary for its violent and unusual pleasures, but when a mysterious gunslinger drags a wooden donkey into the desert town, the stage is set for a bloodbath unlike anything the west has ever seen. Featuring Cthulhu-worshipping Indians, a woman with four feet, a Giallo-esque serial killer, Syphilis-ridden mutants, ass juice, burping pistols, sexually transmitted tattoos, and a house devoted to the freakiest fetishes, Jordan Krall's *Fistful of Feet* is the weirdest western ever written.

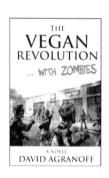

THE
VEGAN
REVOLUTION
... WITH ZOMBIES

A NOVEL
DAVID AGRANOFF

"Dead Bitch Army" Andre Duza - Step into a world filled with racist teenagers, masked assassins, cannibals, a telekinetic hitman, 100 warped Uncle Sams, automobiles with razor-sharp teeth, living graffiti, cartoons that walk and talk, a steroid-addicted pro-athlete, an angry black chic, a washed-up Barbara Walters clone, the threat of a war to end all wars, and a pissed-off zombie bitch out for revenge.

"Necro Sex Machine" Andre Duza - America post apocalypse...a toxic wasteland populated by bloodthristy scavengers, mutated animals, and roving bands of organized militias wing for control of civilized society's leftovers. Housed in small settlements that pepper the wasteland, the survivors of the third world war struggle to rebuild amidst the scourge of sickness and disease and the constant threat of attack from the horrors that roam beyond their borders. But something much worse has risen from the toxic fog.

AVAILABLE FROM AMAZON.COM

Lightning Source UK Ltd.
Milton Keynes UK
UKHW020750040522
402470UK00010B/2185